Grace and Peace,
Penny

The Pauline Epistle

and Other Stories

by

Penny Fritze-Tietz

The names, incidents and characters in this book are the product of the author's imagination, as are all the places with two notable exceptions - the Hagia Sophia in Istanbul, Turkey and Wesley Theological Seminary in Washington, D.C., USA. Any other resemblance to actual events, locales, or persons alive or dead, is completely coincidental.

Second Printing

Printed in the United States of America by

Sunray Printing Solutions, Inc.
25123 22nd Avenue
Saint Cloud, Minnesota 56301

ISBN-10: 1-934478-20-2
ISBN-13: 978-1-934478-20-2

This volume contains three complete Pip Franzen stories:

To all the faithful congregations I have served

(Bethel, Greenwood, Mt. Olivet, Oakland, Crosby,
Deerwood, Aitkin, Silver Bay, Blaine)

The Pauline Epistle

Translation of Epistle found by Pip at family home, 123 Red Pine Drive, and hereafter referred to as The Pauline Epistle.

"Paul, a prisoner for Christ, to Eunice and the saints who gather in her house. Grace to you, and peace, from God and Jesus Christ.

Timothy sends me word of your faithfulness. Linus and Claudia send their greetings and also the greetings of the saints gathered in their household. They praise God for you and for your remembrance of them in their time of trial. Continue to pray for them – that they may be strengthened in Jesus Christ and be faithful in temptation.

My friends from Lystra, saints of the Lord, Jesus Christ, you amaze me! You have taken the Word into your lives and hearts so fully. You live your faith and even send members of your faith household into service of the Word and spirit! I have heard of your messenger, Pauline, in the company of our dear sister, Lois, aged as she is, with only servants in Christ as companions, bringing the gospel of our Lord into all the area, and even the new households of faith in Derbe and as far as Zengma. How proud I am to have been the "father" of these newest churches – or more like their grandfather! The Word of God travels in the hearts and mouths of God's servants, Lois and Pauline. Timothy goes now to encourage them in their faithfulness and to bring them the gifts of love from the churches in Rome and Corinth.

How I praise God for you and your steadfastness. You do not allow the old law to prevent you from living in this new age of love. I encourage you all, dear sisters in Christ, to stand in the strength of the love of Christ.

I remember you in my prayers and also send greetings to Lois, Eunice, Pauline, Sophia, Anna, and to those who are added to your numbers each day. God is surely present in your household. And we praise God for the presence of paracletos! (Feminine spirit of God)

I, Paul, write this in my own hand. I long to be present with you in more than spirit. May the God of love and peace be with you."

Chapter One

123 Red Pine Drive had stood empty for almost a year. We were gathering one last time at our family homestead before it was to be sold. My sister, Marie and her husband Pudge (we were making fudge and he thought we said "Pudge" – it stuck), Bob and Sandy, my brother and his wife (own a resort in northern Minnesota), Don and Sunny, my other brother and his wife (into hi-tech, computer stuff), and the four of us; myself, Lois Penelope Franzen-Fielding, known as Pip, Lanny, officially Lanford Harrison Fielding, III, and our daughters, Kiri and Sarah.

"First of all," said Marie, who is the organizer-matriarch, "we need to clean and make what repairs need to be done before the realtor comes next Wednesday." She promptly handed out a variety of mops, brooms, buckets and assorted cleaning supplies. We each got a list with our "assignment" on it.

"Nothing's changed," mumbled Bob as he and Sandy were dispatched to the basement.

"Oh come on, Bob. This will be fun," responded Sandy, smiling all the way down the basement stairs.

"Don and Sunny, you have the second floor," instructed Marie. Don sharply saluted, pivoted, and marched ever upward to the second floor singing, "Hi Ho, Hi Ho, to work we all must go." Sunny followed, laughing.

"Pudge and I will do the first floor. The kitchen needs the most work," added Marie. "Pip, you and Lanny can do the third floor and storage room. The girls can help you."

I gave a silencing glare to Kiri and Sarah. We took our consignment of mops and buckets and headed for the back staircase.

As far as I knew the house had been emptied of all but a table, one or two chairs, and perhaps a wastebasket or two, so I assumed our job would be a fairly easy dusting, sweeping, and damp mopping the floors.

One-Twenty-Three, as we called it, was a three-storied Victorian farm home built in the days of large families and inexpensive fuel costs. It had large rooms, nooks and crannies, and a front and back staircase. It had been remodeled by my parents to include a large family room, more bathrooms, laundry facilities, and guest bedrooms and bath on the third floor. They had it insulated and re-wired and up-dated the heating/air conditioning systems. It had housed three generations of my family on my father's side. My great-grandfather built it in 1873 when the house, farm and lands had been out in the country. The original five hundred acres has long since been sold, sub-divided, and divided again so that the house now stands on twenty-five acres. It is still surrounded by the lawn, garden and small orchard and stand of hardwoods planted by my great-grandmother.

My parents lived in this house until their deaths, three months from each other, last year. It had been my home and the home of my sister and brothers for all of our growing-up years. It is hard to see it empty and still harder to know that it will be sold.

As I had assumed, the third floor was basically empty. There is one large front bedroom,"empty" checked Kiri and Sarah. The two smaller bedrooms were empty as well. "Not even a dust bunny between 'em," observed Kiri. The hall closet converted to a bathroom was inspected and declared "clean," "neat," and "empty" by the inspection team.

"That just leaves the storage room," I said, and I walked down the long hallway to the door.

The storage room is a large open room at the back of the house. It has three dormer windows, vast closet and storage space, and is a wonderful rainy-day playroom. To enter it you go up two steps the width of the hall-way. I've always wondered why this room was higher than the rest of the third floor but assumed that it had something to do with the fact that it had vaulted ceilings to the actual roof.

There in the middle of the room stood several cardboard boxes of various sizes. As I approached the boxes I noticed each of them was labeled with an envelope taped to the top. As I got closer I recognized the distinctive writing of my father's hand. I opened the one on top labeled "Marie, Bob, Don and Pip." I took the note from the envelope and read:

March 12

Kids,

Your mother and I had such fun gathering these boxes of goodies together for you. There is at least one box for each of you (see labels). They are filled with memories of our life together and our family. We haven't much to leave you in the way of worldly goods, but we can leave you these. They are truly a treasure to us, as are all of you. Enjoy.

We love you.
Mom and Dad

And written as a post-script, these words dated June 1.

Dad has gone to be with God. I won't be long in following. I look forward to a great family reunion. Don't be sad, but glad for me.

Lovingly,
Mom

Mom died on July twenty-third.

As my eyes cleared of tears I noticed that there were, indeed, boxes for all of us.

Kiri and Sarah beat me, just barely, to the stairs as they ran, shouting the whole way, to tell the others of this discovery. Lanny, of course, remained long enough to put the letter back in its envelope and place it on top of the boxes.

We could hear doors slamming, footsteps and voices, all heading toward the family room as everyone gathered. They all spoke at once.

"What in the world," and "we thought someone had been hurt," and "you're as bad as your cousins," (Kiri and Sarah have five equally excitable, equally loud, and equally incorrigible cousins.)

Lanny stood in the middle of the room and called us to order.

"I think you'll want to see what we found in the storage room," he said quietly. He then proceeded to describe and explain what this was all about.

"We're just about done with everything," replied Sandy.

"Yes, so are we," responded Sunny.

"I took care of the leaky faucet in the sink," answered Pudge. "I think we've finished in the kitchen"

We all compared notes and decided that everything had been checked or cleaned or repaired or left alone as needed.

"Let's have lunch first," thought Marie out loud. (I think she was worried about her deviled eggs!)

"That's OK by me," responded Bob.

"Right, then we'll have the whole afternoon to find out what mom and dad have for us," said Don.

"Good idea," said Pudge. We all responded in agreement. Marie set things in motion by bringing chairs, card tables, napkins, utensils and the like from the back porch. Each of us had brought luncheon goodies to share. We set one table with fried chicken, deviled eggs, potato salad, veggies and dip, bars, cookies, fruit salad, ("Mom and her fruit salad!") and homemade lemonade.

As we ate we laughed and talked among ourselves. Sitting on the porch on a warm spring day at "One-Twenty-Three" elicited many vivid and wonderful memories. Most sentences began with "do you remember . . ."

Pudge looked at his watch and said, "Good grief, we've been sitting here for two hours."

Marie and I stood up and while she began to stack the dishes and clear away leftovers I said, "I'm stuffed. Too stuffed to do dishes."

"But not too stuffed to go up to the storage room and investigate boxes," finished Lanny.

"Too right," exclaimed Sarah.

"Let's put stuff that will spoil in the 'frig' at least," suggested Sandy.

We all pitched in and dishes, bowls and trays of leftovers, tables and chairs, were cleared away in no time.

"Do you remember how quickly the dishes got done on Christmas Eve?" asked Don.

"It's sort of like that now," replied Kiri. "I mean, all those mysterious boxes just waiting to be opened."

"Right," said Bob, "and I'm not waiting one minute longer!" and with that he headed toward the back staircase, followed by Don, Sarah, Kiri, and then all of us.

The noise on the bare steps was akin to the proverbial thundering herd. We all arrived at the same time, pushing and shoving as we entered the storage room together. It was quiet for just a moment and then Don said, "Let's do this the same way we did on Christmas Eve."

"Yeah," responded Bob. "The youngest ones pass out the gifts and then we open them, one at a time, from youngest to oldest until we're all out."

We each found a place to sit, not noticing how hard or low the floor was. Sarah and Kiri began to distribute the "gifts." The boxes came in all shapes and sizes.

"OK, that's it," said Kiri, when everyone had their specific boxes. "Mom, you get to open yours first."

My mom and dad knew me pretty well. The very first package I picked up, a yellow manila envelope, actually, had a note on it saying "open me last."

I selected another, opened it, and found it to be full of old school pictures, report cards and papers. Kiri and Sarah jumped immediately on the report cards.

"Hmmmm, 'C's' in math, and wait, here's a 'D' in math. And a note from the teacher, 'needs improvement,'" said Sarah.

"Right, and here's another one, 'is rather talkative when she should be studying,'" read Kiri. Both girls smiled great satisfied smiles. I knew they were charging up their ammunition for another time, another place and other report cards.

Don went next. His surprise was his Captain Scooter Magic Memory Helmet. "I thought this was lost!" he exclaimed, as he stood up and 'flew' around the room shouting magical memory incantations.

After he was done we proceeded to go around the room opening boxes to find still more treasures and surprises from years gone by. There were report cards, class pictures, old toys, letters, and trinkets for each of us. We thought they were long-lost and forgotten.

"You know mom and dad – they saved everything," said Marie.

"I guess they did," said Bob, as he sat in the middle of his set of World War II army trucks. He had a great happy grin on his face.

"Oh, look," said Kiri, unwrapping several piles at the bottom of the box labeled "For everyone, if you're interested."

"Wow," awed Sarah. "Love letters that grandpa sent gramma over sixty years ago."

"And look at these," said Marie. "These are family birth and baptism records. Some of them are over one hundred years old."

We would find an occasional note of explanation taped to the boxes – "Don, your old bike is in the garage," or, "Bob, do you remember this?" (his old football helmet), or "Marie, you have the other one of this, don't you? Now you have a matching set."

After laughter, tears and much conversation we were done.

"All but your envelope, Mom," said Kiri.

"Yeah, open it now," added Sarah.

"Yes, let's see what this mysterious envelope holds," agreed Marie.

Carefully opening the seal I reached in and took out the note.

"Read it," said Sandy.

"What does it say?" said Lanny.

"Hurry up, don't keep us in suspense," added Don.

"Ahem," I cleared my throat.

"Dear Pip," it began.

> "As you may remember from the family stories you've been told, Great Grandpa Franzen (the one who built this house) was a farmer. What you may not know is that he took a degree in New Testament Theology from the University of Turburgen before he left Germany for America. During his years at the University (some time about 1859 – 1863) he spent six months on an archeological dig in Asia Minor. While there he found a small stone jar. The professor and leader of the dig was looking for larger items of some

sort and so without even looking at what Great Grandpa found (can you imagine!?) let Grandpa keep his "little jar" and promptly forgot about it. Some weeks later, when he was alone in his college rooms Grandpa discovered a very old manuscript secreted at the bottom of the jar. He translated the Greek into German (he was a pretty good Greek scholar) and realized what a furor it would cause if it were authentic – or even if it wasn't – and carefully sealed it away keeping it safe for posterity. He married Great-Grandma, came to America, took up farming, built this house, and had a family – you know the rest. What you don't know is that he built a special air-tight compartment in the floor of the storage room where he kept the manuscript. He told his eldest son, my father, of its existence and he, in turn, told me.

It seems to me that it can be no coincidence that you have chosen New Testament Theology as your field of study. I am so proud of you for earning your PhD in Greek New Testament and even more proud of your ordination as an elder in the church. Surely Grandpa Franzen would now agree it was time to bring the "Pauline Epistle" (as he called it) back into the light of the world. You will know how to examine it and you will know who should validate it. You will know how to use it and introduce it to the Biblical world.

One word of caution, from me, but also from Great Grandpa Franzen's words,

> "Be careful with these words, for there will be those who would do anything to keep the world from knowing of them . . ."

And so, Pip, your gift is the greatest of all. Great Grandpa Franzen believed them to be the exact, authentic words of Paul, unusual, extraordinary words of Paul to encourage women such as yourself to take their place in the church in 'the age of love.'

Find the "X" marked in the middle of the floor, count four boards over (going north) and slide the reddish board to the right.

Love from your mom and dad and from Great-Grandpa, too!

March 12

Remember, be careful, sis!"

We all sat in stunned silence.

"Wow," said Sarah. "Do you suppose it's really true?"

"Only one way to find out," answered Lanny. "Find the 'X' on the floor."

We did, indeed, find the 'X', the reddish board, and then the compartment in the floor.

"Look, there it is," pointed Sunny to a carefully wrapped package in the compartment.

"You take it out, Pip. Dad wanted you to have it," said Marie.

"It's all of ours, actually," I said. "We can all share it."

"No," responded Bob. "Dad was right. You should have it. I own a resort, what do I know about old manuscripts?"

"I'm just glad for you to have it," volunteered Sandy. "We'll have the pleasure of knowing about it and knowing that the right person is in charge."

"Yeah, for a pesky little sister you didn't turn out half bad," piped in Don. "You should have it. Just let us know what happens. We'll be proud to have had it in our family."

All seemed to agree.

I carefully took out the package, un-wrapped it, and spread it out on the floor. I couldn't believe my eyes! Before me was what appeared to be a first or second century Greek manuscript. Next to it in a note book of a much later date was the German translation my great grandfather had made along with his notes as to the date of discovery, location, details of the dig, etc. And under the pile was a pair of clean work gloves. I put them on and spread the two and one half pages of manuscript out across the floor.

"Look," I said, "even an original ink blot!"

"Read it! Read it!" cried Kiri and Sarah.

"Well, I don't know," replied Bob. "It's Greek to me."

We all groaned. After a bit of excited conversation we settled down and grew quiet.

"Pip, can you actually read this?" asked Sandy.

"Well, my translation would be pretty rough and I don't want to handle it more than necessary, even with the gloves, although I must say the manuscript is in remarkably good condition. I'll tell you what I can do. Why don't I read to you from Great Grandpa's translation?"

"What good will that do; it's in German?" asked Bob.

What little sister wouldn't take an opportunity like that when it's handed to her. Of course I could read German. It was my doctoral language along with New Testament Greek.

"Sure," I snickered, "I'll read it from the German."

Taking Grandpa's notebook I quickly read in German then translated out loud the text of the long lost letter of Paul.

Chapter Two

The letter itself is quite short. Its impact, however, is great.

"Do you mean to tell me that Paul allowed women to speak?" asked Marie.

"And even encouraged women missionaries?" added Pudge.

Sarah began, "Mom, what was all that about the law, and love, and . . ."

". . . and what about that parakeet thing?" finished Bob.

I read the notes Great Grandpa had written in the margin and re-read the "paracletos" passage.

"Great Grandpa thinks, listen to this, that Paul was well, if not exactly telling a joke, writing an inside joke. After all 'paracletos' is not only the word for Spirit, as in the Holy Spirit, but it's also considered by some to be a feminine word. Hmm . . . women in the church have the last laugh and it's shared by Paul. Not only shall they not remain silent in the church but Paul praises God for the feminine presence of God!"

"Wow," Kiri thought out loud.

"Amen," affirmed Sunny.

Chapter Three

Five months have passed since that day in May when I first read The Pauline Epistle. I took the manuscript to a friend of mine at the American Bible Society. He also is an adjunct professor of Greek at Harvard Divinity School. Once he saw the epistle and shared it with a small group of fellow New Testament scholars, wheels were set in motion that no one could stop.

The manuscript and ink have been tested, dated, analyzed, and tested again. Snytax, vocabulary, and theology have been reviewed over and over by all the tests and experts available. Research has been done on the possible location of the original dig. Translations have been proposed, publicity has been planned and lives have literally been up-rooted, changed and re-scheduled.

Because of my deep involvement with this project I asked for and was granted a leave of absence from my church. Rather than its being sold, my family and I have moved to 123 Red Pine Drive. In September, both Kiri and Sarah returned to their colleges. Kiri to St. Olaf to major in vocal music and Sarah to Beloit to major in Archeology. Lanny has found a new job working for the City of Pine Center, a small, just-beginning-to-grow suburb about five minutes from our home and about a half-hour drive from the suburban sprawl of the metro area.

I have been busily involved in all of the ramifications of being the owner of The Pauline Epistle. This has meant travel to Boston and New York to meet with the various committees. It has included visits to four or five "talk shows."

("Imagine Mom on Oprah!" laughed Sarah.)

Publication day fast draws near and the pace has picked up. There's even talk of a movie! I thought I heard Susan Sarandon suggested to play me!

I also had some time to redecorate and make a home at 123 Red Pine Drive.

After a period of time, about the second week into November, the preliminary publicity had been out, the television appearances were completed and the final drafts for the "accepted for publication" translation were ready, the many letters and phone calls began to arrive. Most of them, to be sure, were words of excitement, encouragement, support, and love from colleagues old and new. There were a few of what I would call typical and expected "crack-pot" responses – you know the type, "communist plot," "anti-Christ," and "tampering with the Bible." Most of those I disregarded.

Chapter Four

There was one letter and one phone message that I took seriously, however. The note arrived in the mail with no return address. It said,

> "There can be no room for you in the church. There will be punishment for those who advocate and sponsor this epistle of the devil.
>
> The True Believer"

As I read the note it seemed to me that hate and venom seeped from the paper. For some reason I had the presence of mind to return the note to its envelope and place them both in a plastic bag which I carefully sealed. I put the plastic bag in my desk drawer, leaving it there for future reference.

That night Lanny and I had dinner out and returned home about 9:30 p.m.

"Pip, the answer-machine light on the phone is blinking. One of the girls probably called. You want me to get it?"

Both Lanny and I walked over to the phone, reaching it at the same time. Lanny pushed the message button. We both stood in utter amazement as we listened to the angry voice speak to us.

> "You won't be allowed to publish your work of the devil. You won't be allowed to lead people astray with your feminist

> blasphemy. Repent of your sins or pay the price of all evil doers. You have one week to retract and withdraw your false writing.
>
> I am
>
> The True Believer"

We both just stood in silence. Lanny made the first move by walking to his chair. He sat down heavily. "Wow, is that for real?" he asked.

"It sure sounds real," I answered.

"Too real," Lanny reacted. He got out of his chair and went to the phone. "We need to call Ed Farnum." Ed is the local chief of police and has become a good friend over the past few months.

"I'm not sure this sort of thing is illegal," I responded.

"Maybe not, but it sure isn't funny or right to do. I'm calling."

It took about ten minutes for Ed to arrive. We greeted him at the door and went into the family room and the answering machine. I also showed him the letter I had received.

"Why didn't you tell me about this?" questioned Lanny.

"Well, I sort of forgot. Besides, one letter didn't seem all that bad at the time."

"I'll get these to the crime lab," said Ed, "and then let you know what we find, if anything. In the meantime, you need to be sure to lock your doors." And, looking at me, "watch yourself, Pip. We really don't know how serious this is but we don't want to make the mistake of underestimating 'True Believer.'" We talked for a few minutes and Ed left with the tape and letter.

Lanny and I talked about the tape and letter for awhile longer and then, "I need some ice cream," he said, and off to the kitchen he went. I, being the dutiful wife, followed.

Although it probably doesn't solve anything, it makes dealing with problems, well, sweeter. That's how our family deals with things anyway. So we sat and talked and ate ice cream. Lanny had chocolate peanut-butter crunch and I had my old stand-by, butter pecan.

"I don't like you being home alone all day while I'm at work," Lanny said.

"Lan, you have ice cream dripping from your moustache," I

responded.

"Never mind that, we need to figure out how we can keep this nut from doing something dangerous," he answered.

We talked some more, finished off the ice cream, turned off the lights, and went to bed.

"Did you lock the doors?" asked Lanny.

"I thought you did," I answered.

Lights came on, covers were tossed, the cat was moved, (not a pretty picture) Lanny left the room heading downstairs. I heard mutterings, a crash as the chairs got bumped, more mutterings, and then, as Lanny came back into the room, he made THE PRONOUNCEMENT.

"From now on we'll keep all the doors locked, day and night. We'll use our keys and mostly go in and out the back door. All the windows will be locked, too."

I lay awake for quite awhile thinking about all that has gone on in our lives since May.

"Pip," Lanny reached over in bed and gathered me in his arms, "I am worried about this."

"I know, Lan, and I think maybe I have a plan. You know Pudge is going to be on active duty for the next few weeks. Marie said that he's going to do some flight-training review stuff for some of the National Guard units. He'll be at one of the bases in Florida. (Pudge is a colonel in the Air Reserves and often returns to duty to teach "refresher courses" for the National Guard.)

"I'll call Marie tomorrow and ask if she would be willing to come and stay for awhile."

"Good, Marie would be perfect, if she'll do it!" responded Lanny.

We talked about the girls and how they were doing in school and then, as so often happens, we'll be in the middle of a conversation, Lanny will be saying something and in mid-sentence, silence, followed by a snort-snore. Lanny can fall asleep mid-syllable.

"Good night, Lan," as I leaned over and kissed him.

"Humph," he answered.

Chapter Five

I picked up Marie from the airport.

"What we have to do," she said, after our initial hellos, "is make sure we have a good security system. I've called two different companies for estimates. Here's their brochures – I think this one is the best, what do you think?"

"I don't . . ."

"Well, Pudge and I talked about it. We like this company," (indicating one brochure). "They said they could be out this afternoon at 3:00 p.m." Looking at her watch, "Good grief, let's get going. We've got a lot of work to do before then."

And so we have a security system at 123!

I put Marie in her old room, just kitty-corner from the master bedroom on the second floor. I'd been able to get some of the old furniture out of storage. While she was visiting I thought we could paint that room and freshen it up a bit.

"I thought you might like some hot chocolate and cookies," I said, as I knocked on her door. "I know you are tired but maybe you'd like to relax a little before you go to sleep."

Marie and I sat cuddled up in the two comforters from the old twin beds.

"It's good to be here again," she said.

"We're so grateful that you came," I answered. "Lanny was worried, and I must admit, I'm a little nervous, too."

We talked about the 'True Believer,' plans for the days ahead and The Pauline Epistle.

"Is it really all that revolutionary?"

"Well," I said, "probably not to a lot of folk in mainline churches anymore. After all, most of them have women involved at every level of church activity. But just suppose you're a male pastor in a male-dominated church or sect. And let's say you've been justifying your dominant stance with the passages from Paul that say women shall remain silent in the church, and so forth. Along comes 'Pauline' – poof – there goes your argument, your authority, and your control."

"Yes, and your power," whispered Marie.

"But enough to kill for?" she continued.

"People have killed for a lot less," I answered. We both shivered.

"Who would be so threatened by this that they would send those hate messages to you?" she asked. "Can you think of anyone?"

"I hate to think that anyone would react this way but someone has."

As if by some unspoken agreement we stopped talking about it.

"So, how are the girls doing in school?"

I gave a quick run down of classes, activities, recent boyfriends, and a general review of life in academia.

"When will Pudge be done with his duty?"

"It depends on a couple of things. A group of officers are talking about doing some fishing after classes are over. I'm guessing he won't be home until the first of December at the earliest."

"Which means you'll be with us for Thanksgiving?" I asked.

"I thought maybe I would be but I don't want to inconvenience you if it doesn't work out," she replied.

"Absolutely not! We'll have a house party! The girls will both be home and now you, too!"

We talked about and began to plan for Thanksgiving. Nothing pleases Marie more than to have something to plan! We were in the midst of a serious discussion of pies and pie crusts when Marie looked at her watch.

"Goodness, its 1:30! If we're going to get up and shop tomorrow we'd better get some sleep."

"Goodnight," we both said. I walked across the hall to the master bedroom. Lanny was comfortably snoring in sleep. Next to him on my side of the bed was our orange marmalade cat named Webster.

"Webster, move over, you're in my place," I urged.

He looked. No movement.

"Come on cat, move or get squashed."

Nothing.

"OK, you asked for it," I said, as I climbed into bed, dangerously close to cat claws.

"Come on, move over, Webster," I ordered again, knowing that one does not order a cat to do anything.

"Meow, fssst, growl," and then, slash!

"Ouch, you darn cat!" I bellowed.

Lanny rolled over, gathered Webster into his arms and said, "Would you stop pestering the cat, please, Pip!"

I'm sure the cat smiled.

Chapter Six

We shopped 'til we dropped. A week later we went one more time to get the curtains for the spare bedrooms on the third floor. We finished our shopping, curtains in hand, and were on our way home when we heard sirens.

"Oh, no," I thought out loud. "I always worry when I hear them. I wonder who it is and what happened."

As we stood in the parking lot of the mall we saw the lights flash and turn the corner.

A minute or so later as we approached the car Joyce Freeman, our neighbor to the left, and her teenaged daughter, Terrie, ran up to us and said, "Oh thank goodness you're all right. We saw the accident – somebody in a huge black van broadsided a car and just drove off. We were about twenty feet away."

"We saw the whole thing," added Terrie, excitedly. "The funny thing was that we had just waved at the lady in the car because she looked just like you."

"Yes," Joyce continued. "The car was an exact duplicate of yours, right down to the box of Kleenex in the back window."

Marie and I smiled at what was a family trait picked up from our dad.

"I could have sworn the lady was you, Pip," said Terrie. "She held her head the same way you do. I even heard her radio from the open window – it was classical music!"

A dead give-away, to be sure, I thought, then realized what I'd been thinking.

"We're sure glad it wasn't you. See you." And with that they left to go to their car.

Marie and I looked at each other for a moment.

"Are you thinking what I'm thinking?" she asked.

"No, couldn't be," I said, shaking my head.

Chapter Seven

Later that evening I got a phone call from Ed Farnum.

"Pip, I don't want to alarm you but I think that 'True Believer' has done more than just write notes and leave phone messages. Have you got some time? I'd like to come out and talk with you."

He was there in about twenty minutes.

"There was a hit-and-run accident today just outside the mall. The car was an exact duplicate of yours. The license plate was 396 MTY (mine is 396 MKY). The woman driver looks very much like you. I just don't think it was an accident."

"What are the chances of that car being so much like mine," I wondered to myself, and out loud I asked, "What happened to the woman in the car, Ed?"

"I'm sorry, Pip, she died shortly after arriving at the hospital. Whoever hit her car wasn't fooling around."

Ed and Marie were talking together. My mind took me elsewhere. Although I had not driven the car that caused the death I still felt an overwhelming sense of guilt and disquiet. I spent several moments trying to work this through to some place of satisfaction. I had just about worked through the guilt to a sense of outrage and indignation that such an unnecessary death should occur when I heard . . .

"Does this mean that 'True Believer' thinks that Pip is dead?" asked

Marie. "If so, maybe Pip should stay out of sight for awhile and see what happens."

"Yes, and in the meantime we need to discover the identity of 'True Believer' and bring this nonsense to a halt." I replied.

"How do we do that?" Marie asked. I could tell I had sparked her curiosity.

"Easy does it," replied Lanny. "You two can get into enough hot water without being involved in a real nut-case murder."

"I know my department is small," said Ed, "but I can call in some favors from the state crime lab. Let me carry the ball on this."

"Oh, sure," and "Yup, good idea," from both Marie and myself.

Ed left after assuring us he would keep us apprised of further developments.

"You're up to something," Lanny speculated.

"Well not yet, of course. But in a way I feel responsible. After all, that woman was killed because they thought she was me."

"We don't know that for sure, Pip. It could actually have been an accident," answered Lanny.

"Possible, but not likely," muttered Marie.

Chapter Eight

The next morning around the breakfast table we talked a little more about Thanksgiving.

"Will Don and Sunny and their kids be coming this year?" asked Marie.

"I talked with Sunny a couple of days ago and she and Don will be here but the boys will both be at their in-laws. She said she'd bring her usual salad, a pie and some of her homemade pickles."

"What about Bob and Sandy? Can they get away?" continued Marie.

"Same thing with their kids. Bob and Sandy are planning to arrive here late Wednesday evening. Don and Sunny should be here Wednesday about noon. I thought Sunny said something about going shopping at the mall for Christmas presents."

Lanny groaned. "More shopping! I thought we were going to simplify this year!"

"Who said I was going to shop?" I asked.

"I know you. If Sunny goes you'll have to help her find all the right stores and all the good bargains and then, as long as you're there, you might just as well pick up a little something for good ol' who's it."

"Hush," I said. "Good ol' who's it might be you, you know."

"What's Sandy bringing?" asked Marie, ever-ready with her list in hand.

"I think she said she'd bring a couple of pies, some rolls, and cookies, nuts and munchies for the game."

"That means we need to have the rest. I'll make a list," said Marie.

"Of course you will," Lanny responded, and quickly left for work.

"Now that he's gone, let's get down to the real stuff," suggested Marie. "What are we going to do to solve this mystery?"

We sat down and, you guessed it, made out a list of things to do and questions to ask.

"We need to talk to Joyce and Terrie Freeman and see if they can remember anything more about the accident. Then we need to ask around and see if anyone says anything that could help us."

Marie was up and ready to go.

"One last thing," I added.

"Yes, what did I forget?" asked Marie.

"The grocery list."

"Oh, yes."

We paid a visit to Joyce and Terrie.

"It all happened so fast," said Joyce. "We were coming out of The Gap . . ."

". . . I need some new shirts for school," added Terrie.

". . . When we saw you drive past . . ."

". . . We thought it was you. It sure looked like you, ah . . . you know, your smile, your wave . . ."

". . . The Kleenex in the back, and the radio playing classical music . . ."

". . . right, I mean you're the only living person I know who listens to classical music," added Terrie.

"I do," answered Marie.

"Really?" responded Terrie in astonishment.

"And then what happened?" I asked.

Joyce answered, "It was frightening. One minute you, or at least we thought it was you, drove past and the next minute this huge black SUV broadsided your car and drove off going about 50 miles per hour. I still see that horrible picture in my dreams."

"We called 9-1-1 on my cell phone," continued Terrie. "I mean, wow, I've never done that before."

"Several people were there. I remember one man saying, 'give me room, I'm an EMT,'" added Joyce.

"He tried to help the woman but I guess she died later at the hospital," said Terrie.

"Then we left after the police arrived and took our statements," said Joyce. "We couldn't really be of much help except that we saw a black SUV."

Marie and I asked a few more questions and then left.

"That's not much help," she said, "but I still have a 'gut' feeling that:

It was no accident and

It was meant to be you in that car."

"Let's think about this for awhile," I said. "Besides we have Thanksgiving to take care of."

"Maybe something will come to us," added Marie. "There's more to 'True Believer' than a nasty note and phone call."

We went grocery shopping – two-and-a-half carts worth!

"I don't know, I feel like we've forgotten something," speculated Marie.

"The turkey?" I asked.

We groaned and went back into the store.

"Don't tell Lanny," I requested. "He'll never let me forget it."

Marie solemnly promised.

Chapter Nine

Wednesday morning before Thanksgiving and the house was a-bustle. Both Kiri and Sarah had arrived the night before; Sarah by bus and Kiri with a friend who would also be spending Thanksgiving with us. ("It's alright, isn't it, Mom? Karl's family is so far away and they don't really 'do' Thanksgiving, and . . ." Karl was from up-state New York. He seemed to be very nice and fit in well. We put him in the guest bedroom on the third floor.

Grocery shopping for last minute supplies, making beds (Bob and Sandy in the third floor green room, Kiri and Sarah in their room on the second floor, Don and Sunny in the blue room on the second floor), and cleaning bathrooms ("Why do I always get this job?" asked Kiri) and vacuuming and dusting ("Kiri has it easy, she only has to do the bathrooms!") of the family, living and dining rooms.

In the midst of the flurry Don and Sunny's car drove into the driveway. The traditional family rush to the door, greetings, hugs, and "everyone carry something" occurred as Don and Sunny made their entrance.

"Say, Pip," mentions Don. "Who's big, black van is that parked at the end of the driveway?"

"Yes, we almost hit it as we came in. Who in the world would park their car right in the middle of the road?" added Sunny.

Marie and I both said we didn't have any idea whose it was but we wished that we did.

"Has it been there long?" Don asked.

"No, this is the first I've known about it," I replied.

"Well if it gives you any trouble by parking there, you let me know. I'll go chase them off," Sarah enthused.

"Right, and how would you do that, Whimpie?" questioned Kiri.

This was followed by a lively discussion of "who's Whimpie," and was carried out into the backyard where it erupted into a free-for-all leaf battle and escalated into a family running, jumping and making noise contest.

The kitchen had been emptied of all but Karl and me. He asked timidly, "Is your family always like this?" To which I replied, "No, Karl, sometimes we're worse!"

He looked surprised and then we laughed.

"Incidentally," he added, "I don't know if it makes any difference, but after breakfast this morning I took a little walk around the neighborhood. I saw the van, too. It was parked off the street in that little cul-de-sac down the block. I'm sorry I'm such a nut about things like this. My mom says I'm exasperating, but, well, I memorized the license plate."

Karl gave me a small sheet of paper on which he had written the make, model and license plate number of the black SUV.

"Thank you," Karl. You're not a bit exasperating. This is just exactly what I needed."

Chapter Ten

We gathered together around the big table in Grandpa and Grandma's dining room. We ate, we talked, we laughed. Each one remembered something special for which they were thankful. We prayed and sang together. We had turkey with all the trimmings – mashed potatoes, gravy, dressing, cranberries, squash, rolls, pies and still more.

The weather was wonderfully mild with temperatures in the mid 50's. We played a quick game of football – yes, I can still catch a forward pass. It was a grand day for giving thanks.

Evening came. We had cold turkey sandwiches, fruit salad, hot chocolate, apple and pumpkin pie and more conversation around the fireplace in the family room. And we were thankful for all that was ours.

Early Friday morning I could hear footsteps and muffled conversations in the hall. Webster and I ignored them as we cuddled under the warm comfort of the bed covers. Lanny was sound asleep and didn't hear a thing.

Crash! I did hear something! I hastily put on my robe and slippers and followed the noise to the kitchen. Kiri, Sarah and Marie were busily engaged in mixing up pancake batter, making French toast and scrambling eggs. Bob, Don, Sandy and Sunny were all seated around the table in various stages of dress looking like Oliver Twist asking for more gruel.

"We wondered when you'd wake up," said Sarah. "We've been up for hours."

"Yes," added Kiri. "Aunt Marie had us spy on that black van at the end of the driveway."

"And we found out quite a bit, I must say," replied Marie. "Let me tell you all about it."

"Maybe later – everyone doesn't have to know about this, do they?" I whispered to Marie.

"Too late," answered Bob. "We already know."

"Yes, we're all in this together," said Sandy.

They all nodded in agreement. Then Marie filled me in.

"First of all, the van is rented under a false name and address. Ed Farnum already checked that for me. Next, we've put the van under constant surveillance. That's where Karl is now. We're on half-hour shifts."

I groaned.

"But Karl is a guest in our home. He doesn't want to get involved in some crazy scheme like this," I protested.

"That's where you're wrong, Mom," answered Kiri. "Karl thinks this is cool. His family just eats out for Thanksgiving and then sits around and watches football."

"We could learn a lot from them," I mumbled to myself.

"Right," said Don, not hearing what I said, "while in our family we eat, play football, eat, try to apprehend crooks and weird-os, eat, catch spies, and, oh yes, did I mention that we eat?"

During this conversation everyone was eating – passing plates of bacon, sausage, eggs, pancakes, and French toast around, generally having a good time.

"I thought I smelled food," said Lanny, as he entered the kitchen from the back stairway. He was greeted with, "here, sit down," "have some sausage" and "those pancakes are pretty good," etc.

The conversation switched back to the black SUV. Lanny was filled in on the information and with several not particularly fact-filled theories.

As we were talking, the door opened and Karl staggered in. His face was bloodied and dirty, his clothes were ripped and soiled.

"What in the world happened to you?" we all asked and then "here, let me help you," and "someone get some band-aids."

While I went to get wash cloths to clean his face and bandage him, the others proceeded to help him with his jacket and outdoor things. About ten minutes later we determined he had no serious injuries. We calmed down and were ready to hear his story.

"I was hiding in the bushes when you left (indicating Marie and Kiri). I stayed there for awhile but decided that I could probably get closer if I was careful but then as I got closer, the side door of the van shot open and two dark figures jumped at me. They were yelling and screaming about a she-devil and evil-doers. While they yelled at me, they hit me with some big black book. Then they got in the van and drove off."

We all sat in stunned silence. And then, "People actually do these kinds of things?" mused Sandy.

Karl, rubbing his head responded, "You better believe it. And, oh yes, one more thing. It's not all bad, you know. I got something out of this beside a bunch of torn clothes and some bumps and scratches. As they were hitting me one of them lost this." He held up a W.W.J.D. bracelet. "Look, it even has someone's initials on it."

We all groaned. No one wanted to embarrass and disillusion Karl. Who had the heart to tell him that W.W.J.D. was short for 'What Would Jesus Do?,' a popular "buzz" phrase among many younger Christians.

"Wait," exclaimed Sarah. "There really are initials on it."

I looked at the bracelet. The letters were on separate squares of silver. On the back of the last square in very small engraving, was written:

"In memory of J.E.P.,
Christmas, 1995"

I slipped it into a plastic bag, sealed it and said, "Hopefully there are still some fingerprints on it. We'll have Ed check it for us."

Everyone had some comment and as the volume of noise rose, Karl stood up and said, "And I also grabbed this just before they got away."

Karl took it out of his pocket and, carefully unfolding it, laid it on the table. It looked to me as if it were the front dedication page that was often found in the front of big pulpit Bibles. It said,

> "Given to the Bostwick Methodist Church to the Glory of God and in honor of James E. Peterson, on this June 14, 1961, by his friends."

And in the corner of the page was written in a different hand and ink,

> "Bostwick Church closed on September 1, 1961, rather than be served by a woman pastor.
>
> Signed,
J.E.P.
A True Believer"

"Wait a minute, just a minute," I thought out loud. "I remember hearing something about this. I had just graduated from high school and was at a Conference youth meeting just before I went to Mitchell (South Dakota) to go to D.W.U. (Dakota Wesleyan University). There was a big stink about some little church that got in trouble because they refused an appointment. They were tiny and about all that was left was a handful of members. They were very loyal to their former pastor who had served the church for twenty years, or maybe more."

"I remember that," said Marie. "I was teaching in the town next to this little town of Bostwick. They were going to put it on a circuit with our little church and one more about ten miles from us. They refused and one day the D.S. (District Superintendent) came and the church was locked and there was a sign on the door that said,

'Church closed – we
Obey God's Word not
(wo)mens!'"

Chapter Eleven

Saturday came. Lanny had to work the weekend. Bob, Sandy, Don and Sunny had made plans to visit mutual friends for the day and then go home from there. That would leave Marie, Karl, Kiri, Sarah and me with no particular schedule.

We'd just finished breakfast. I hugged Lanny good-bye about the same time Bob, Sandy, Don and Sunny were ready to leave.

"Good-bye," we all waved.

"See you at Christmas?" asked Sunny

"We'll call and let you know what's happening," I responded. "I hope we can all get together."

Further hugs, good-byes, waves, and last words and they were gone.

"Bye, hon," said Lanny and was out the door.

"I can't believe he left without saying good-bye to his cat," said Kiri.

"You're so jealous of that darn cat, Kiri," responded Sarah.

"He does spoil it pretty bad," answered Kiri.

Just then Webster raced across the kitchen from the garage going toward the living room.

"Look, he's even got a smug look on his face. Lanny must have said good-bye," said Marie.

"Meow," said Webster.

"I'll take that for a yes," said Sarah.

"So, what should we do today?" asked Kiri.

"I was thinking about visiting some of my old friends at Towerville," replied Marie. "It's just about the right distance for a pleasant day's trip."

"Yeah," answered Kiri, "we could go to the deli and pick up some stuff, or maybe even make sandwiches . . ."

"Turkey . . ." interrupted Marie.

". . . have a picnic, you know, make a day of it," finished Sarah.

"Towerville," I mused. "Isn't that the little town about five miles from Bostwick?"

"Hey! Bostwick! Isn't that the church that doesn't like women ministers?" added Karl.

"You catch on real quick, Karl," answered Marie, as she nudged first Kiri, then Sarah.

"Well, let's get going," they both responded. They began by slicing turkey and making sandwiches and putting together a banquet picnic.

We were ready to leave in forty-five minutes. As we packed the van (Lanny drove the car since the woman had been killed in one just like it) Marie stood at the door and checked off her list. (I did say she was organized!)

"Sandwiches, pickles, olives, cheese, potato salad, chips, apple pie slices, fruit salad, Dr. Pepper, fruit juice, deviled eggs, brownies . . ."

"Good grief, to do think we'll have enough to eat?" I asked. No one was listening. The list continued.

". . . Flashlight, mace . . ."

"Mace?" I said.

"Hush, Mom," said Sarah.

"Twine, first aid kit, cell phone, camera, video camera, hair spray . . ."

"Hair spray?! What the . . ." I asked a little more vehemently.

"Quiet, Mom. Aunt Marie says hair spray is a really good defensive weapon to surprise someone with," explained Sarah.

"She would know," I responded sarcastically. I got glares.

"What in the world . . ." I continued.

"Oh Mom, you never know what . . ."

". . . or who," continued Kiri, "we might find."

"Aha," my mind fitting in the last piece of the puzzle, "we're going on a little fact-finding mission," I said.

"Well of course, what else," replied Kiri.

"Come on, get in, Mom. We're ready to go," instructed Sarah.

"I'll drive, I know the way best," said Marie.

I sat in the backseat. Marie drove, Kiri in front with her, Sarah and Karl in the middle seat, and I was in the back seat with all the "supplies." I could see, hear and feel the excitement as the "Red Pine Investigative Committee" conversed, planned and schemed.

"Hold your horses," I objected. "We can't just walk in and start pointing fingers at people."

"We know," answered Karl.

"Right – we're just going to look around and ask a few questions," said Sarah, quite innocently. They turned and smiled reassuringly at me.

"Just go to sleep like you usually do when we drive, Mom," soothed Sarah. Although she didn't touch me, I could feel the motherly pat on my head.

I was not amused.

I was not reassured.

Chapter Twelve

Actually it was a very pleasant drive. We left about 9:00 a.m. and arrived in Towerville at 11:15 a.m.

"I don't think anyone I know is still here," said Marie, "but let me check one place." With that she parked the van in front of a typical-looking home-town diner and coffee shop. The paint-chipped sign read, "Hannah's."

"I'll just be a minute," she added, and went into the little café.

About fifteen minutes later she came out with a smile on her face and a bag of home-made doughnuts. The wonderful aroma of those doughnuts wafted through the air and brought me out of my post-travel trance. I immediately perked up and was able to take nourishment.

Marie had learned a good bit about the "Bostwick church group" from her friend Hannah McDaniel. Hannah was the cook, baker and owner of the restaurant. She was also quite an interesting story in her own right. And she also made wonderful doughnuts!

"It seems that people from around here have been reporting strange things happening at the old Bostwick church," she explained.

"What are we waiting for, let's go see for ourselves," exclaimed Kiri.

"Yes, let's do it!" said Sarah.

I wasn't about to say too much because I had a mouthful of doughnuts but I did gesture my caution.

"Your Mom's right, girls," answered Marie. "We'll be very careful . . ." which was not exactly what I meant but no one seemed to notice.

Too late! I realized that they had already made their plans. We were going to the Bostwick church as long-lost family members visiting the cemetery and reading and making rubbings from off of the oldest tombstones.

"So what are the strange happenings at the Bostwick church?" asked Karl.

"It seems that there is an awful lot of traffic in and out of the church, lights on late at night, and noises," responded Marie.

"All this from a supposedly abandoned property does sound a little suspicious." ventured Sarah.

"Hannah says that the church picnic grove and cemetery used to be a pretty popular lover's lane for the local teenagers. But since about two months ago, the teens have stopped going there – too much noise, traffic and lights on and off for a lover's lane, she says," continued Marie.

"Maybe we shouldn't be trespassing on private property. We could get in real trouble," said Karl.

"We could get in real trouble because of what's going on," I said, "but not because it's private property. You see, in our denomination all church property is only held in trust by the local church. All real property belongs to the Annual Conference. And I happen to know that the Bostwick Church and cemetery are still the property of the Minnesota Annual Conference and are not someone else's private property. I've been asked by the Conference Board of Trustees to come out here and inspect the property preparatory to its sale. In other words, I'm actually one of the few people who have the right to visit the church. As a matter of fact," I reached into my purse, "here's the key to the front door." I held up an old-fashioned brass key.

"Mom, you old rascal," laughed Kiri. "You were planning to come here all along!"

We all laughed and, getting into the van, drove off to inspect the former Bostwick Church.

"I guess you have the last laugh, Mom," mused Sarah.

I thought of 'True Believer.'

"We'll see, Sarah. We'll see."

Chapter Thirteen

We drove the five short miles out to the Bostwick Church. Hannah was right – it made a pretty good 'lover's lane.' It was a one-lane gravel road, twisting and turning into the open countryside.

"It's kind of pretty out here," remarked Kiri.

It was indeed a beautiful drive. The road followed a small stream. "That's Wild Rose Creek," pointed out Marie. The stream flowed into a small, clear lake. "And that is Rose Lake," continued Marie.

"This would be a great place to camp," said Karl. "I wonder if there are any camping areas around here."

"If it's this pretty this time of year, imagine how nice it would be in the summer," speculated Marie.

As we rounded the bend we saw a white steeple.

"That's it," said Sarah. "I can see the church from here."

The church was set on a little rise at a bend in the road. It looked to be the stereo-typical white country church complete with stained glass windows, steeple, picnic grove and cemetery. All in all, quite charming.

We pulled into the grove and parked.

"This is nice," said Kiri, jumping out of the van.

"Smell the fresh air," added Marie.

"Oh, Aunt Marie, you're just like Mom. She 'smells' everything," responded Sarah.

"That's true. When we were little, Mom had us out in the woods smelling the trees, the rivers, the wild flowers, everything," said Kiri. "Our friends thought we were goofy."

"We Franzen's do go by our noses, I guess," Marie answered.

We walked up the steps to the front door. I unlocked the door and we went in. It really was a lovely little country church. There was a center aisle with six rows of pews on either side. The front, or chancel, of the sanctuary had a pulpit in the middle and the communion table pushed back against the wall. On the table there were brass candle holders, candles and a large open pulpit Bible.

"I was right! It's opened to the Twenty-Third Psalm," exclaimed Kiri.

"Oh, you're not so smart," muttered Sarah. "They always are."

"But look at this," said Karl, turning the Bible to the front pages. "It looks as if a page has been torn out."

"Does it match this?" I asked, taking the page out of my purse.

"That's the page that Karl grabbed when he got jumped," exclaimed Kiri.

We laid it across the torn page of the Bible.

"Looks like a match to me," speculated Marie.

"Hmmm, why would anyone carry this big, heavy, cumbersome thing in the first place?" asked Sarah.

"Right, and why would they try to clobber me with it?" continued Karl.

"I suppose they wanted to share the Gospel with you," I laughed.

"Not funny, Mom," returned Kiri.

"Not funny, perhaps," retorted Marie, "but I think there's probably some truth to what your mother is saying."

"I wonder if maybe whoever attacked you, Karl, and whoever is threatening me isn't on some kind of mission for God, at least in their own mind," I wondered out loud.

"You mean like hit 'em hard with the truth and they will come?" asked Sarah.

"Something like that," I nodded.

"That's weird," said Karl.

"So weird it could be true," murmured Marie.

"OK Mom, oh great detective, what else have you noticed," asked Sarah.

"One thing – remember the Franzen propensity to 'smell?' I almost said something to you when we first came in the door."

Both Kiri and Sarah began to sniff the air, although it was obvious to me, at least, that it was sarcastic sniffing.

"Come on, Karl," coaxed Kiri, "smell, smell!"

"I believe the grammatically correct way of saying that would be 'sniff, sniff!'" corrected Sarah. "As in I sniff, you smell."

"Or," Karl, going in, "I smell, you stink."

"I do not," retorted Kiri, indignantly. We all laughed.

"You see, Marie, it's no use," I said. "You can't take the children anywhere."

After a moment Sarah replied, "OK, Mom, tell us what we should know."

"There are several visual clues," I answered, "but you were right the first time, it was the smell that gave it away. Listen and learn, meine kinder. Number one, when we came in, I smelled coffee."

"Oh, come on, Pip. Even I know that every Methodist church this side of heaven smells like coffee," cited Marie.

"After over thirty years of being abandoned? Not even Swedish egg coffee lasts that long!"

"Next, what I didn't smell."

I could see Kiri and Sarah's noses twitching. I continued.

"I didn't smell must. An old wooden building, locked up all these years should be really musty and dusty smelling. And lastly, I smelled candle wax."

Our eyes turned to the candles on the communion table.

"You're right, Mom," declared Sarah. "These are pretty new."

"They should have broken, melted away, or simply be gone by now, if they'd just been left," Karl commented.

"You know, now that you mention it," said Marie, "this place is remarkably dust free." She wandered up and down the rows of pews, running her fingers over the backs and sides.

"Aunt Marie would notice that," said Kiri. "No one dusts and cleans like her."

"No one in our family, anyway," said Sarah.

Aunt Marie is the acknowledged 'clean machine' in our extended family.

"It's pretty clear to me that this sanctuary is being used on a fairly regular basis," I concluded.

"Let's check out the basement," suggested Sarah.

"Right, and then after we've done that we'll need to take some pictures of the whole place," I said.

We walked back to the front entry door and went down the stairs to the basement.

"Look, Mom," pointed out Kiri, "they have a food shelf."

We walked over to a cupboard shelf filled with items of canned and packaged foods.

"I'm afraid churches thirty years ago didn't have food shelves," I answered.

"That must mean someone's been here," concluded Kiri.

"Yeah, a lot, I'd say," said Sarah.

"Even slept here," called out Karl from a small room off of the larger one. "Look, I found a couple of sleeping bags and some other stuff."

We continued to look through the basement rooms, finding much evidence that this building was being used fairly frequently. Karl was busy taking pictures with the Polaroid camera and Kiri was labeling them. Sarah moved about with the video camera and Marie was busy cataloguing what she found.

"It doesn't really look as if this has been used for any church-type purposes," she said. "I don't see any Sunday school material or stuff like that. And I wonder what's with all the charts and maps on the walls?"

We spent a few more minutes in the basement and then returned to the main floor sanctuary to take pictures of that, too.

After fifteen minutes or so I said, "I guess we've got enough of what we need. Let's go see about eating that huge picnic lunch you packed."

The weather was wonderfully warm and mild; it must have been in the high fifties or low sixties. We backed the van next to one of the old picnic tables in the grove and set out our lunch.

As we ate, we talked of what we had seen in the church.

"I don't get it," said Karl. "What is going on here?"

"Me either," Kiri responded. "The sanctuary looks as if somebody's having worship services in it but the basement doesn't look like a church basement at all."

"Yes, more like a command post of a military campaign," said Marie. "I've seen them like that on TV."

"It seems strange to me, too," I said. "There's more here than a possible connection to The Pauline Epistle."

As I spoke a vintage black 1955 Buick Roadmaster drove into the driveway and parked next to the church. Three 'old-lady types' got out and slowly crossed the yard to where we were having our picnic lunch.

"Who are you and what are you doing here?" asked the tallest one.

"Now, Maud," said the shortest one, we really don't need to be rude, do we dear?"

"Well, they're trespassing on private property," Maud answered, although I noticed that she backed off a step or two and seemed to get a little shorter.

The middle lady responded, "Maud, Agatha is right," and to me she said, "We don't mean to be rude but we are sort of the guardian watch-dogs of the church here."

Kiri and Sarah were about to speak up when I glanced at them to keep quiet. I've learned that often times the best way to learn things is to remain silent and let the other person speak, particularly when they seem to be a bit nervous. I call it 'over explaining' (like I'm doing now!). I know it worked well with two teenage daughters!

Karl, Marie, Kiri, Sarah and I all remained silent. The three ladies didn't seem to notice our lack of response.

"Hettie," this time Maud was speaking, "I'm not sure we're exactly watch-dogs – more like care-takers. We keep the sanctuary clean and ready for worship. You know when Rev. Peterson was alive he always liked the way we cleaned."

"And I was the best altar guild member in the whole church," glowed Agatha.

"You were the only altar guild member, Aggie," retorted Maud.

Their conversation went back and forth between the three of them almost as if we weren't there. After about five minutes of listening to their reminiscences of by-gone days and dear Rev. Peterson and all the quilts they'd made ("I still think the blue log cabin we made for Bessie and Albert had too much green it in it."). They began to speak about the "committee" and was it possible that they'd gone too far in frightening that women down in the 'Cities.'

I intervened.

"What woman was that, Hettie?" I asked.

"Why you know," she answered. "The one they accidentally hit with their van and afterwards they parked by her house and watched her for awhile."

"Yes, that was the time they got attacked by the group of hippies who tore out the front page of our Bible," continued Aggie.

"They also stole the bracelet you gave me to remember Rev. Peterson. I'd given it to them to have it fixed at a jewelry store. Remember, Maud, I'd asked that nice Tom fellow to take it and get it fixed."

"No, Aggie," responded Maud. "You didn't ask Tom. He told you he'd take it and get it fixed for you. As I recall you hadn't even realized that it needed to be fixed. Something or other about the clasp."

"Oh yes, I remember now," Aggie answered.

"I still think it was too bad that they ran into that woman and smashed her fender," added Hettie.

"Wait a minute, wait just a minute," commented Sarah. "You mean that you think this Tom person accidentally hit some woman . . ."

"Not just <u>some</u> woman," replied Maud. "They hit that Pippy Franzen-Fields person. You know Tom told us about her. She's a woman's-libber, ah, libertine woman, who wants women to rule the church. It's too bad they had to hit her but after all she's going against God's will and really should go home to her family."

All five of us stood with our mouths open.

After a moment of amazed silence Marie spoke, "Wouldn't you ladies like to join us for a light luncheon?"

Sarah and Kiri took the hint and added their invitations as well.

I said I hoped they didn't mind being so informal but that we'd planned a picnic.

"Yes, nice homemade potato salad and pie," continued Marie.

"Pie?" responded Maud. "Oh my goodness, Agatha, Hettie, don't you think we might stay?"

And so they did.

When they asked how we happened to be there we explained about the tombstone rubbings which seemed to amaze them to no end.

"Lots of people do it now days," said Kiri. "It's a good way to get in touch with your family tree."

Hettie, Agatha and Maud thought that was a good idea.

"Tell me," I asked in between bites of turkey sandwiches and fruit salad, "do you ladies live near here?"

"Oh yes," answered Maud. "We're sisters you know and we live around the turn in the road, just past the church!" She pointed to where the road disappeared beyond a bend in the road.

"And did you all go the church here at one time?" asked Karl.

"Why I should say," answered Agatha. "We were all baptized here and . . ."

". . . And I for one plan to be buried here as well," replied Hettie, emphatically.

"But the church looks closed," said Marie. "How would that be possible?"

"It won't be closed for long," smiled Maud. "We have a plan."

"Or rather Tom and his friend, Robert, have a . . ."

Just as Hettie was about to say more Agatha 'shushed' her. All three women had their hands over their mouths.

"Oh, dear, perhaps we've said too much already," whispered Maud.

"Where did you say you're from, dear?" asked Hettie.

Marie jumped in with "I'm from Milwaukee. Just here for a quick visit to the cemetery. I have some long-lost great somethings or other buried here," and then quickly, "won't you have some more pie?"

Conversation dwindled for awhile as we watched our guests devour pie. As they ate Hettie and Maud seemed to be having their own silent debate over something. Agatha watched for the length of time it took her to eat a slice of apple pie, then said,

"Oh, alright, you two, I'll tell. I've been bursting with it for the last two weeks and these seem to be nice trustworthy folks."

"Homemade pie wins again," whispered Marie to no one in particular.

"We're so excited," began Agatha. "We'll be able to attend church again and we won't have to worry about any of that new fangled stuff that they have over at the M.E. Church in Towersville."

"M.E. Church?" questioned Kiri.

"Methodist Episcopal," I answered. "Merged in the 1930's. Old percursor to U.M.C. You can ask me later," as I nudged her to silence.

"But how can you be buried in a church that's closed, it isn't even yours?" asked Sarah innocently.

"But it is ours, dear heart. We own it lock, stock and, well, pulpit!" declared Maud.

"But Mom said . . . ouch, that hurt!" responded Kiri as both Marie and Sarah silenced her somewhat abruptly. "Oh, I get it."

"Dear Rev. Peterson saw to it that someone responsible would take care of this property," continued Hettie.

"And who is more responsible than we are, I ask you," said Agatha.

"You own the church?" I asked pointedly.

"Yes siree-bob," responded Hettie. "We own the church, the cemetery and the fifty acres that they sit on. I have the papers in my drawer at home."

"And it's so fortunate that the church property and our land are right next to each other. We've put all the land together into one," said Agatha.

"Tom suggested that. He's been so helpful," added Hettie. "We have two hundred acres, oh yes, and the pond, stream and lake, too." She concluded, "Quite a lovely piece of land for a church."

"And in just a little while we'll be able to begin holding Sunday services," said Agatha.

"And Sunday evening hymn-sings on the lawn. I just love those old services. And I've missed them so," said Maud. "But of course we can't hold the hymn sings until next summer."

And then turning to me she added, "That's what your lovely picnic has reminded me of. Thank you so much."

"Maybe we'll be able to have some ice cream and pie socials," commented Hettie. "I have a wonderful recipe for gooseberry pie I haven't used for ages. Not since I was seeing Art Johanson from over in Towerville."

"My dear, that's at least fifty years ago," reminded Maud. "He's long gone by now."

"Well, he did like my pie, don't you remember, Aggie?"

"Yes dear, we all liked your pie."

"But Art liked it fine, I guess," said Hettie. "He liked me fine, too, until that woman doctor came along and snatched him from me."

Agatha patted her gently on the arm and Maud leaned over the whispered to me, "She's not been the same since it happened, poor dear."

We all nodded sympathetically. I stood up and said I thought we'd better gather things together as we had a long ride home.

We packed up the remains of the lunch and sent left-over pie home with the ladies. As we were about to drive off, Marie asked, "You don't suppose we could see the inside of your lovely church, could we?"

The three women looked at each other.

Maud said, "Tom and Robert warned us not to go in for anything but Sunday service but, well, I would so like to show it to you. Perhaps for just a moment or two."

"But we've already seen . . . ouch, you don't have to pinch so hard, Kiri," Karl said, holding and rubbing his arm. "Oh, I get it."

"What dear?" asked Hettie.

"We've already had lunch," adlibbed Karl.

"Yes, my dear, and such a nice time we had," said Maud.

"And now we're going to pay a special visit to these ladies lovely old church," emphasized Marie.

"Yes and perhaps they'll be so kind as to tell us a little bit about it. I know I'd love to have as much information as possible," I added.

Karl's eyes lit up. "Gotcha."

Chapter Fourteen

Agatha took a big brass key from her purse.

"What a neat, old-fashioned key," observed Sarah.

"Yes it is, isn't it?" She unlocked the door and we went into the sanctuary. "This key," holding it up for all to see, "is the only one left, I believe," explained Agatha. "Even Tom and Robert have to ask to be let in and out."

"They think they're fooling us, but they aren't. We know what they're up to." They all smiled and nodded knowingly.

"And what do you think they are up to?" I asked.

"We don't think, we know," answered Agatha, secretively.

"Let me tell you, dear," said Hettie. "I do so enjoy telling a story."

"I'd better tell," responded Maud. "After all it was my idea."

And without waiting for Agatha or Hettie's approval continued.

"You see, we think that these two young men are planning to start their own church."

"Oh yes," interrupted Agatha. "They always seem to be talking about God and Jesus. Why every other word is God!"

"Indeed yes," continued Hettie. "I think they are a bit heavy on hell and damnation, as well. I do hope they ease up on that. After all, no one wants to be damned or sent to hell with every last sentence they hear."

I was so amazed at what I heard that I had to keep my eyes down. I could hear Kiri and Karl snickering and felt that Marie and Sarah were holding their sides.

"Well anyway, my dears," continued Maud, "I believe Tom and his friend think they've found a place to start their church. I heard them talking about it one day not too long ago. Something like the church of the Resurrection Resort and Health Spa, whatever that means."

"I'm not sure we just want to hand over the deed for the church grounds and cemetery that dear brother Peterson gave us. I'm not convinced Tom and his friend are spiritual enough to lead a church," she concluded.

"We did sign over the property to them in trust, in case something should happen to us," said Agatha.

"I know, but that won't be for years and years," reflected Hettie. "We're in the prime of life."

"All except my lumbago, of course," remembered Maud. "And of course there's Agatha's little problem with her bladder . . ."

"Hush, Maud," said Agatha.

"Yes, I guess the less said about that the better," answered Maud.

"Let me see if I have this straight," said Marie. "You have a deed to this property . . ."

"Yes, Rev. Peterson had a fancy one all made up for us," explained Agatha.

"But Mom, you said . . ."

"Hush, I believe Agatha was explaining to us about their deed," I said, hastily.

"Rev. Peterson gave us the deed and the only key to the church with the instructions that we never let a woman defile the church . . ."

"Wait a minute," asked Sarah. "Aren't you women?"

"Oh dear, now don't confuse me," said Agatha.

"Be still, Sarah, and let her finish," I said. "We'd really like to hear her story without interruption. You were given a deed and the key to the church. Why you?"

"Why that's simple, dear. We're the last ones left!" exclaimed Maud.

"The faithful three, that's we!" giggled Hettie.

"What happened to Rev. Peterson?" asked Kiri.

"He's gone these twenty-five years, now," answered Hettie. "We had his funeral in this very church. He's buried in the Peterson family plot just beyond the pine grove."

"That's where we'll be, too, Hettie, 'when we go.'" said Maud.

"I think I'm beginning to understand," I said. "Come on, folks, we need to be heading home."

We walked toward the front doors.

"Oh wait," I said, "I think I left my bag downstairs," and quickly went down the basement stairs.

But Mom, I have your bag . . ."

"Come along, Sarah," Marie out-maneuvered everyone and quickly led them to the car.

I returned from my expedition to the basement.

Good-byes were said by all. I can still see Maud, Hettie and Agatha standing on the front steps of the church, waving good bye with their lace handkerchiefs, the last of a dying breed.

Chapter Fifteen

We were quiet for the first few miles, lost in thought of what we had heard and seen.

Then Karl asked, "Are those three for real? Could it all be an act?"

"It almost seems as if they're caught in some kind of time-warp," answered Sarah.

"I think you're right," said Kiri. "They certainly aren't of this age."

"More likely fifty or sixty years ago," responded Karl. "They've been untouched by the new millennium."

"So now what?" questioned Sarah.

"Let's go home and sort out one or two things," I suggested. "This is a pretty drive."

I could tell the rest in the car were exasperated by my seeming indifference to the whole situation but I had to take some time to think through everything. I needed to mentally step back and look at the whole picture.

Besides, a little cat-nap wouldn't hurt, either.

Chapter Sixteen

We arrived home about 7:30 p.m. after making the usual pit stops. And, of course, one Dairy Queen stop.

Lanny was seated in the family room, cat on lap, television remote control in hand, watching yet another football game. He was eating leftover turkey and dressing.

"I'm glad you're here," he said. "I'm ready for some pie and ice cream."

"Can't you get it yourself?" asked Kiri, as yet un-versed in the ways of keeping a happy and balanced marriage.

"I have a cat on my lap and he's so comfortable. It would be a shame to have to move him," he responded.

Webster looked up at us and smiled.

"I'll get it," I said. "I wouldn't want to inconvenience the cat." I also don't mind serving my husband.

We settled in for the evening. Everyone found what leftovers they wanted. We all had plenty to eat as we gathered in the family room. After the football game (Packers 27, Chicago 17) Lanny said he was going upstairs to bed.

"You people might be able to stay up and party but I'm a working man. I have to be at work tomorrow at 5:00 a.m. We are starting on that water filtration plant project."

I went up with him. Webster came upstairs as well and found a cozy spot on the bed.

Lanny and I talked for awhile about his work. The city water treatment plant was being inspected and Lanny was involved with that. He took his job seriously and was always the first one at work and the last one to leave. Lanny is 'Mr. Reliable" to my Ms. Impetuous." All-in-all, a good man to have around.

We talked a bit more. I told him of our trip today and shared the information I had learned with him. I could see how tired he was so I tucked him into bed, kissed him goodnight and turned off the light. As I came down the stairs I could smell popcorn and a wood fire in the fireplace.

"We left the butter and stuff to you, Mom," said Sarah. "You do it best."

"You make the very best popcorn around," added Kiri.

"Do you want regular popcorn or caramel corn?" I asked.

"Regular," responded Kiri and Sarah.

"Caramel," answered Marie.

"What's the difference?" asked Karl.

While Karl got filled in on the family story of Grandpa's caramel corn (the secret is to cool it with the Sunday funny paper. Really!) I fixed the two batches of popcorn; regular with lots of melted butter and salt and caramel, made with the secret old-family recipe (I can't be bribed!) and cooled with last Sunday's funny paper.

"Mmmm, this is good," munched Karl.

"It's all in the wrist action with the funnies," said Marie.

"How does that have anything to do with how this tastes?" asked Karl, somewhat bewildered.

"Don't know," answered Sarah. "It's just a family tradition."

"Our family doesn't have any traditions," said Karl. "We just work at making money."

"We have tons of traditions," said Kiri. "No money, just traditions!"

We talked for awhile about some of them as we munched on our popcorn. (Sitting around the fireplace telling stories, popcorn, playing football, singing together, family vacations, laughing and telling jokes,

Christmas Eve, and lots of others.)

"Remember how Granpa Franzen got a box of chocolate covered cherries every year for Christmas? He never knew who sent them."

"Yeah. Granpa hated chocolate covered cherries! He said it was a waste of good chocolate," remembered Sarah. "We all ate them. One year our dog, Nutmeg, ate them. We thought she'd get sick and die. But she didn't. She loved them."

"Yup, every year that mysterious, wrapped box would show up. Who gave it to him, I wonder?" asked Kiri.

Marie answered, "It's a mystery, a deep, dark family mystery." You could tell that Marie knew more than she was saying.

"And speaking of mysteries isn't it time you shared your ideas with us about what happened today, Pip?"

"Right, Mom, it's time to come clean," said Sarah.

"Yes, what was all that about leaving your bag in the basement? We hadn't even been in the basement with the three little ol' ladies," questioned Karl. "I'm surprised they didn't ask you about that."

"I was hoping they wouldn't notice," I said. "I remembered some charts on the basement walls. I wanted another look. So here they are," and I walked over to where I keep my purse and pulled some large, rolled sheets of paper out of it.

"Remember Maud mentioning 'Resurrection Resort and Health Spa?' For Maud and her sisters anything connected to that property must be a church, right?"

They nodded.

"So Resurrection Resort and Health Spa must be some kind of, in her words, new-fangled church."

"It makes sense in a weird sort of way," commented Marie.

"Now look at this chart," I continued. "It's a pretty detailed map of the church, cemetery, grove and the sisters' adjoining land. And look on this next one." I shifted some of the pages, "there is super-imposed a large building complex."

"It looks like it might be big enough to be a hotel," speculated Karl.

"Right on the first guess," I said. "This is prime real estate for a resort."

"So that's what this is all about," mused Marie. "A whole big plot to

. . . to what, Pip?"

"Here's how I see it. If Tom and his buddy, Robert, can implicate the three sisters for murder . . ."

". . . That would explain the hate mail and nasty stuff that's been sent to you," said Marie.

"Sure, and also the murder of mistaken identity," pondered Sarah.

"All on the mistaken assumption that the church and its land . . ."

". . . Along with the three sister's land as an added bonus," added Kiri.

". . . Would come to them after Agatha, Hettie and Maud are out of the way," finished Karl.

"It's really simple, isn't it?" asked Kiri.

"Sure, once you know what's going on," responded Sarah.

"OK, what's our next move?" asked Marie.

"The best thing we could do would be to tell Ed Farnum all this and let him take it from here," I emphasized, strongly.

"Not good enough, Mom," retorted Sarah. "This is our case."

"Right, so what is our next move?" asked Kiri.

I gave in. After all, it couldn't hurt anything to theorize, could it?

"The same as it always is, proof-evidence. We have the motive so now we need to prove our case," I answered.

"We even have narrowed down the suspects," said Kiri.

"But have we?" asked Marie. "I mean this is all very well in theory but we haven't even met the mysterious Tom."

"You think he's a figment of their imagination? What if it really is the three old ladies?" questioned Sarah.

"Yeah, right. They jumped out of their van, having left their old Buick on the farm, and beat up Karl," commented Kiri, sarcastically.

"Well then, three very determined old ladies. No wait, I know. They're not little old ladies at all. They're three escaped convicts on the lam . . ." continued Sarah.

"Not aliens from outer space sent to turn all churches into cosmic way-stations?" I whispered, to myself, of course.

"Mom . . ."

"Get a grip, Sarah," cautioned Karl.

"OK, so it was three little old ladies . . ."

"I may not be in the greatest shape but I think I probably could take those three old ladies in, well . . . at least two out of three," reasoned Karl.

We were all silent for a moment and then we each began to laugh, quietly at first, trying not to hurt Karl's feelings, then snickers, giggles and out-right belly laughs.

Marie apologized. "I can't help it. The vision of Karl going to the mat against our three little old ladies just strikes me so funny."

"Me too," said Kiri. Even Karl was laughing. We sat talking and laughing as we finished up the popcorn. I looked at the clock.

"Good gracious, is it that time already?" It was indeed 12:30 a.m. We had spent the whole of the evening in conversation and speculation.

"I'm going to bed. This ol' lady needs her rest." I yawned.

"But Mom, we right on the edge of solving this thing," complained Sarah.

"We can't go to bed until we put the wraps on this mystery," furthered Kiri.

"Oh yes I can," I said. "See you in the morning – err, make that later in the morning."

And off to bed I went.

Marie followed suit.

"We should stay up and solve this thing once and for all," stated Sarah.

"Oh come to bed, Sarah. I really am tired," said Kiri.

"OK, not much point in me being up by myself." And as Sarah began walking toward the stairs she added, "Wait, one more piece of turkey for the road."

"Good idea," seconded Kiri.

"I was hoping someone would think of it," added Karl.

I heard sounds of the refrigerator door opening and closing, microwave noises, the clatter of dishes, all lasting for another few minutes.

"Mmmph," muttered Lanny. "I smell food. Is it time to get up?"

"Go back to sleep, dear. It's just the hordes of vandals and visagoths attacking our food supplies." I patted him on the head, kissed him on the cheek and tucked him snuggly under the covers.

"That's alright, then," he mumbled. "Just so it's not serious."

The cat meowed and rearranged himself on my pillow.

Lanny lovingly reached over and patted Webster on the head. "Good night, honey," he said.

I am loved.

Chapter Seventeen

Morning brings clarity. Didn't someone say that once?

In our household morning usually brings that chaos commonly referred to as breakfast.

Lanny got up and was ready to go to work but, "would you mind fixing me some eggs?"

As I fixed his eggs (over easy with toast and juice) the cat begged for water. Not just any water, mind you, but water from the cold water tap and then his dish must be hand-held for him at a certain place at the table. As Lanny holds the cat's water (I apparently don't hold it correctly) Marie came downstairs and joined us in the kitchen.

"I thought I'd make some pancakes if that's alright with you."

"Sure, fine, all the stuff for pancakes is in that cupboard," I said, pointing to the cabinet next to the refrigerator.

Marie busied herself with making pancake batter. Webster was still lapping his water.

"If the cat has finished, your breakfast is ready, hon," I said.

"You pamper that cat way too much," said Marie. Marie has never had a cat.

"No argument there," I respond.

Webster then jumped off the table and ran for safe-cover just as the heavy footsteps of the proverbial thundering herd are, well, heard.

Sarah, Kiri and Karl all entered in various stages of dress. They have sleep in their eyes and hunger on their lips.

"How about some French toast?" suggests Sarah.

"Good, I'd love some," answers Kiri.

"Are you making it, Mom?"

"Don't forget we've got pancakes," reminds Marie.

"Oh, goodie. Do we have some of that good sausage from 'The Barn?'" (naming a Mennonite farm-store we often frequent.)

"How about some maple syrup? Oh, I know, do you still have some of that apricot syrup I like?" asked Kiri.

"You forgot eggs," I added sarcastically. "Doesn't anyone want some eggs?"

"Sure," they responded. "We'd love some to go with our sausages, pancakes and French toast." Sarcasm is lost on them.

In the midst of this Lanny finished his eggs, got up and gave me a good-bye hug and started off to work with the words, "Stay out of trouble, Pip."

I gave him my sweetly innocent look – it had never worked before but who knows, maybe this time!

He responded with, "Don't think I don't know what you're up to," and left. Webster ha-rumphed as only a cat can, and left the room.

"So, Mom," said Sarah, in between bites of eggs, sausage, French toast and pancakes, (how does she eat it all, I wonder?) "What's up for today?"

"You know I've been thinking that we need to go back to the Bostwick church and set a trap for Tom and his buddy, Robert," suggested Marie.

"Just what I was thinking," said Karl.

"Me too," piped in Kiri. "And we need a plan, a really good plan."

"And I was thinking that this would be a really good time to bring all that we know to the attention of Ed Farnum," I said.

"Not that again," groaned Sarah.

"Yes, again," I interrupted, "I think Ed and the police are the one's who should take it from here."

Chapter Eighteen

Ed had good news and bad news. Yes, he was interested in our little theory. Yes, he agreed it made pretty good sense. Yes, he had authority over the investigation of Betty Jane Hill's death (the mistaken identity 'hit and run').

No, he couldn't just cross several county lines and arrest suspects without further evidence.

"The trail is cold, Pip," said Ed. "I've had to treat Ms. Hill's death as a hit-and-run accident. Unfortunately we have no witnesses or leads. The van that hit her hasn't been found."

"You must admit that our speculations make some sense," coaxed Marie. "After all, the make of car and even the license plate similarity are awfully coincidental.

Ed nodded his head, "Tell you what I'll do. I know the sheriff of Landis County. He ought to be familiar with the Bostwick Church. Maybe he can come up with some information as well."

"I guess that's a start," I answered. "Thanks, Ed, I appreciate your willingness to help. I know it sounds a bit far-fetched."

After Ed left, we got to the serious business of lunch. We headed over to Lanny's office to see if he would take us to lunch.

"All of you?" he exclaimed.

"We won't eat much," whimpered Sarah.

"Hah!" was all he said. He did, however, go to his desk and take out his checkbook.

"Well, come on," he said, and walked across the street to Penny's Diner and Emporium.

Seated around the large family table in the front window we began the serious task of ordering our lunch.

"What's good?" asked Karl.

"You're in small town Minnesota, my boy," commented Lanny in his W. C. Fields imitation, "Everything is homemade and good here. Personally I'm having a hot hamburger sandwich with mashed potatoes and gravy, and, for my vegetable, a piece of chocolate cream pie."

"That sounds good, but I think I'll have the fresh fruit plate with a cup of French onion soup," said Marie.

After much discussion and many changes of mind, lunch was ordered and served. We settled down to the business of eating and mystery solving.

"Here's how I see it," I postulated. "Tom and his friend, Robert, know a good deal . . ."

". . . a scam, it's a scam," corrected Kiri.

"Yes, alright, a scam, when they see one. They schmoozed their way into the good graces of our little ol' ladies in order to get possession of the church and the land it sits on. They believe, as do Hettie, Maud, and Agatha, that the ladies own the rights to all of that very valuable property."

"How does any of this connect with The Pauline Epistle?" asked Lanny.

"It doesn't really, except that Tom and Robert must have heard the women talk about it. They probably said what 'Dear' Rev. Peterson would have thought about it. They heard about the Bostwick Church being closed and its refusal to accept a woman minister. They put it all together and built a circumstantial case against the ladies, carefully planting the clues that we found to incriminate Maud and Hettie and Agatha. With their conviction the pathway to owning the property was clear."

"That's right," remembered Karl. "The ladies did say something about leaving their property in trust to Tom."

"But the plan backfired. They didn't kill you, Mom, they got Betty Jane Hill, instead," said Kiri.

"No matter," I replied, "They quickly went to Plan B. Although I suspect I'm still on their 'most wanted' list as long as a capital crime was committed, they hope to implicate our little ol' ladies by plan or by accident, in murder."

"What do you think the property is worth to a real-estate developer?" asked Sarah.

"Millions," Marie answered. "Lots of millions."

"What's our next move?" asked Lanny.

"<u>Our</u> next move, Lanny?" questioned Marie. "I thought you didn't want to have anything to do with this."

"You don't think I'd let you go back to that church unprotected and defenseless, do you?" he replied.

"So," he repeated the question, "What's our next move?"

"Pay the bill, dear," I said.

Chapter Nineteen

As it happens our next move was pretty obvious. Other than waiting for Ed Farnum to solidify his case and bring charges against the unknown hit-and-run driver, we decided to return to the Bostwick Church and confront (catch, trap, ensnare, whatever) Tom and his band of a crooked man.

Lanny needed some time that afternoon to tie up loose ends at work so we decided to start early Monday morning for Bostwick.

"Actually we don't start classes until Thursday so we don't have to miss any school," both Kiri and Sarah assured me. Karl didn't have classes until the following week.

"How do they learn anything if they never have to go to class?" asked Lanny. No one had an answer. I thought it was a pretty good question, however.

We went to church on Sunday. Kiri sang a solo and Sarah read the Scripture lesson. Lanny taught the adult Sunday school class. I preached the sermon so the pastor could have Thanksgiving weekend to go home to her family in Wisconsin. At the last minute the organist called and said she had a bad case of Montezuma's Revenge; she was sorry, she couldn't possibly play as she couldn't get past the bathroom. And did I know of anyone who might play.

Marie was a music major at Hamline. Marie played the organ.

"I don't believe this," said Karl. "My family goes to church for Easter and an occasional family funeral. My mom has to threaten my dad with death to get him to go even then. You all seem to like going to church!"

"Yup, we do!" answered Kiri. "Church is part of our extended family. Every Sunday is a family reunion!"

"You don't understand, Karl," said Sarah. "That's what we do – church. It's in the genes of this family."

"It's a little more than that, Toots," I replied.

"I guess it's who we are," continued Sarah.

"It's what we believe," concluded Lanny.

We had Sunday dinner – roast pork, mashed potatoes, gravy, creamed peas, fried applies, salad, and homemade ice cream with Marie's famous frosted sugar cookies.

Sunday dinner activities were another new experience for Karl. In our family the children do the dinner dishes.

"I've never done dishes in my life," he said. "It can't be all that bad."

Lanny, Marie and I sat in the living room relaxing as we listened to the clatter of dishes being washed and then dried and thrown across the room to be put away, another quaint family tradition.

As I dozed off (still another family custom!) I could hear Lanny and Marie talking softly. I just barely remember hearing Marie saying, "But what if we're wrong?"

Chapter Twenty

That evening I received a call from Bob Whitemore, curator of the Museum of American Script (on the University of Minnesota campus). I had placed the original Pauline Epistle there for safe keeping. Bob called to inform me that the museum had been vandalized. The Epistle was safe – they'd only gotten some copies of it, but they were checking the vaults and security systems to be sure it would remain safe.

"The vandals left some writing on the walls. Something about 'doing God's will not (wo)mans' and signed 'The True Believer.' They did some mischief-type damage to one or two of the displays. We'll take care of security here, don't worry about it. Just be sure you're safe, Pip," he added, just as he hung up.

"That settles it," said Lanny. "We need to get to the bottom of this, and soon."

I went to bed but I could hear them all in conversation together, low and serious, making plans.

Chapter Twenty-One

Monday dawned cold and crisp. We got up early, had breakfast and packed the van, all with a minimum of conversation. I watched as the odd assortment of goodies and gadgets everyone thought we would need were packed into the back of the van and overflowed into the seating area. I was about to ask what everything was for but decided to remain silent when I saw the looks on their faces. These were people on a mission!

We were going to Bostwick!

The drive was pleasant enough although we were a bit crowded what with all of the extra 'equipment' everyone had packed.

As we turned into the driveway of the church out of the corner of my eye I saw movement and lights going out in the basement of the church.

"I thought I saw something," I said.

"Me, too, Mom," replied Kiri.

"If someone is here we'll have to watch our step," reasoned Lanny, as he parked the van next to the church.

We all got out and started toward the front door.

"You go in, I'll just stay out here and see what I can see," instructed Lanny. "And incidentally, don't get yourselves in trouble in there."

Lanny isn't particularly a large man but he is solid and strong. It was just a moment's hesitation and then I agreed. "OK," I said. "You be our back-up man."

He nodded. "I always am." He held my eyes for a brief moment and then it was time. I took the key from my bag, unlocked the front doors, and we went into the church.

The church seemed pretty much as it had been on our earlier visit. We looked around and finding nothing new of interest on the main floor, descended the stairs to the basement.

"Yes, indeed, the basement. The nest of the whole operation," whispered Karl.

"What in the world are you muttering about?" asked Sarah.

"Ssssh . . .," whispered Marie, as she put her hand over Sarah's mouth.

"Oh, right, quiet," she said through Marie's fingers.

As we entered the large area of what was the fellowship room we saw the food shelves, bed rolls and stacks of papers we had seen before. It looked as if someone had added more papers. There were also some shirts and socks scattered about.

"Whoever they are, they aren't very neat," reflected Marie.

From behind one of the larger cabinets a tall, slim, blond male, aged about thirty, emerged and said, "If we knew you were coming we would have cleaned up the place."

As I turned to look at him another man, average height with red hair and a large gold University of Minnesota sweatshirt, stepped behind us, pointed a gun in our direction and said, "Actually, we were kind of expecting you. We knew a nosy dame like you (pointing his gun at me) couldn't pass up the opportunity to snoop around until you found something. Your snooping has played right into our little plan."

"Wait a minute, you can't go waving a gun at us and . . ."

"Hush, Kiri!" I nudged her. "Let's hear what Tom has to say."

"So you know my name, huh. Well that's all you're going to get from here on in," he responded angrily. "Now all of you get over here," he gestured to us and pointed his gun toward a small room off the larger one.

"Come on, get moving," the other man pushed Karl and Sarah.

"Hey, stop it, I'm moving!" exclaimed Karl.

As we entered the room Marie said, "Hettie!"

"Agatha," said Sarah and Kiri,

"Maud," said Karl, "What are you doing here?"

"It's obvious, isn't it," replied Tom's partner, whom I assumed to be Robert.

"You came to Bostwick to confront these three little old ladies . . ."

"We are not old," scorned Maud.

Yeah, right, whatever," said Tom.

Robert continued, ". . . and you got into an argument, had a bad, bad accident and the church caught fire and you all perish in a horribly tragic mistake."

"So sad," added Tom.

"Incidentally, you can all call me Robert, but not for long, of course," he laughed.

Hettie, Maud and Agatha were bound at the wrists with what looked to be a long neck scarf. They appeared to be more frightened than hurt. And they were more angry than frightened.

"Land sakes but I'm upset with you, Tom," said Agatha. "I just can't believe that we could make such a mistake about someone."

"But we surely did," continued Maud. "My stars but we were wrong in our judgment of you."

Hettie just stood and glared.

"Shut up, you old broads," said Robert. "You talk too much and too funny."

"No," replied Tom. "Let them talk. It could be quite informative. Like where is the original copy of the deed?"

"Yeah, talk ya ol' biddies," growled Robert.

"Well, I never . . ." retorted Hettie.

"Hah, maybe you should-a," shot back Robert, nastily.

"It seems as though you have a slight problem, what with not having the deed," I mused.

"Shit, we'll find it. It's got to be somewhere in their house, it's for sure not in this building. All we've found so far is this (holding up three sheets of illuminated, printed pages) stuff. It's fancy alright, but it sure as hell ain't legal. No matter, we'll have lots of time to find it after you're gone," grumbled Robert.

"But that is the deed," exclaimed Maud. Hettie and Agatha quickly cautioned her to silence.

"The deed's not going anywhere. We'll have plenty of time and opportunity to find it," nodded Tom.

"True, right after the big, sad fire," taunted Robert.

Maud, Agatha and Hettie huddled closer together. They alternated between fear, anger and indignation.

Meanwhile, instead of huddling together, Karl, Kiri, Sarah and Marie had quietly spread out around the room. Tom and Robert seemed not to notice.

"The truth is, ladies," Tom addressed the three sisters, "you made it so easy and inviting to scam you that we couldn't resist."

"The truth! My word but you haven't a shred of truth in either of you," exclaimed Maud. "You ought to be ashamed of yourselves."

The three ladies drew themselves up to their full heights.

"And now you've involved this nice family from, ah, Wisconsin, wasn't it?" said Agatha.

"No ladies, I'm afraid this 'nice family' has misled you, too," answered Tom. "It seems as though no one is really who they say they are."

"Oh, dear, I'm so confused," said Hettie. "Who is who and what is what?"

"Rev. Peterson would know," asserted Maud. "He always knew what was what."

"Actually, it's Rev Peterson who, at least in part, got you into this mess," I explained.

"Oh no," whispered Hettie. "Rev. Peterson was a man of God. He knew what was right."

"Come one, let's get this over with, we've waited long enough," urged Robert.

"We waited all these months, we can wait five more minutes," reasoned Tom. "Besides, we might learn something about Rev. Peterson and that could help us find the . . ."

". . . The deed," interjected Robert. "OK, let's listen."

"Tell us what we need to know about Rev. Peterson," asked Tom.

"Well, Rev. Peterson was a dear, sweet man who . . ." began Hettie.

"Not you, I meant her," said Tom, pointing at me.

"What is it you want to know?" I said, stalling for time.

"You seem to know about this Peterson guy. Maybe you know where he put the deed."

"Actually, I never met the man," I answered. "But I do know a little about how things in the church are done."

"What the hell do we care about that," retorted Robert, angrily. "Get on with it. She's stalling."

"Am I?" I answered. "Well then, why don't you tell me where the deed is?"

"I ought to slug you," responded Robert, menacingly. He started to cross the room toward me.

Tom stopped him and leaned toward me, "Well, do you know where it is?"

"My stars above," muttered Maud. "Of course we do. And didn't Rev. Peterson hand it over to us just a month or so before he died. And isn't that it in your . . ."

"Hush, Maud," cautioned Hettie. "They don't need to know."

Robert walked over and raised his hand, about to hit her.

"Wait!" I said. "You really need to listen to what I have to say."

"You haven't said much of anything yet," growled Robert.

"Yes," said Tom. "I'm getting impatient with all of this. Tell me what you know and make it snappy," and with those words he pointed the gun at me.

"It's like this." I moved to sit on a chair in front of the sisters. I motioned to Tom to sit on a second chair. Surprisingly he did. As he sat I noticed that Kiri, Karl and Sarah had moved so they were standing right behind and to the side of Robert.

I continued.

"Several years ago this church was served by a lay-pastor by the name of James Peterson . . ."

"Our dear Rev. Peterson," whispered Agatha.

"Anyway, James Peterson was sort of a maverick. He was a retired school teacher turned part-time preacher who found himself a congregation to preach to. Bostwick was a little church that couldn't afford a full-time minister. Peterson fit the bill. He managed to get himself appointed here."

"Yeah, yeah, get to the important stuff," demanded Robert.

"As I was saying, Rev. Peterson became the resident pastor and sometime 'saint' of the church. Unfortunately he was pretty vague about the denomination he served and began to believe that he was the sole authority. He began to make some pretty outrageous claims and set up some rules that were pretty outlandish, according to our United Methodist Discipline. Sorry, ladies," gesturing Hettie, Maud and Agatha.

"He was relieved of his appointment and another pastor, a woman, was appointed to serve Bostwick and Towerville and Birch Pond churches. Rev. Peterson was incensed and convinced the few members who were left at Bostwick that women should never be allowed to preach from the pulpit and specifically from 'his' pulpit here at Bostwick."

"Mom, you know more about this church than you let on," said Sarah, in amazement. "How much more do you know?"

"Rev Peterson was surely upset about a woman minister," reflected Hettie.

"I'm beginning to get the idea that maybe it wasn't a woman preacher that upset him as much as his being told to step down from this church," Karl said, thinking out loud.

"So he told everyone he was retiring and convinced them to lock up the church under protest of women in the ministry," guessed Kiri.

"That's about it," I answered.

"Oh dear, oh dear," muttered Maud, "But is it true?"

"And here we've been without a church for all these many years, why?" asked Agatha.

"There were only ten members at the time so the Conference simply voted to close the church," I added. "And now we get to the point of this – where you come in," I indicated Tom and Robert. "In our denomination all the property is held in trust by the local church but belongs to the body we call the Annual Conference. The reason you can't find the deed is because it is in the files at 122 West Franklin Avenue in Minneapolis, the Conference and corporate offices of the Minnesota United Methodist Church, which owns the building and all the properties related to the Bostwick Church."

"But we have the deed!" said Maud. "You saw it," pointing to the papers Tom had laid on the table. "And we have the only key to the church."

"You may have some kind of deed-like papers," I said. "Unfortunately your Rev. Peterson, at the least, misunderstood and, at the most, got greedy or sneaky about Bostwick Church and its properties. I'm sorry, ladies."

"But the key. I still have the only key," said Agatha. "Surely that means something."

"You mean like this one?" I asked, as I pulled the key I had out of my pocket. "I really am sorry that you were so misled. The Bostwick Church never really belonged to Rev. Peterson to give to anyone. Therefore, if you don't own it you couldn't possibly pass it on . . ."

". . . To me," said Tom. "I've been out-shystered and out-scammed."

"What a rip-off," complained Robert.

"Tell that to Betty Jane Hill," Marie muttered.

"I won't be cheated out of a big bon-fire," Robert yelled. He reached into his pocket and took out his lighter.

"It's pay-back time. You ladies are roasted," and as he was about to set the room on fire, Karl shouted to Kiri and Sarah,

"NOW!"

Karl, Kiri and Sarah grabbed Robert from all sides and held him down. As for Tom, well, he faired no better. Marie placed a karate kick square on his jaw and I knocked the gun from his hand. In the excitement of the moment Lanny came in, and with twine in his hand, made sure Tom and Robert were securely tied.

"What took you so long?" asked Sarah.

"I was looking for the twine that you packed way in the back, under everything else in the van," he replied. "Besides I could see you had everything under control."

Chapter Twenty-Two

We met upstairs in the sanctuary. Hettie, Agatha and Maud sat together very much subdued. Kiri, Sarah, Marie and Karl all sat together in the second pew, behind the three sisters. Lanny and I were in front by the communion table.

"I'm sure glad that sheriff came when he did," said Karl. "How do you suppose he knew when and where to come?"

"I think you can thank Lanny for that," I responded.

Lanny smiled and held up his cell phone.

"But you never use it!" sputtered Kiri. "We gave it to you last Christmas and you thanked us then put it away in your drawer."

"When it comes to new-fangled gadgets, well that's what you call them, you don't need them, you said," added Sarah.

"Sometimes I don't like a lot of extra fancy, high tech stuff," Lanny explained, "but I do use this cell phone every once in a while at work. And it came in handy today!" he beamed proudly. "I called the sheriff just as soon as we got here. Actually, he was expecting my call. Ed had made arrangements with him. We talked about it before we left home."

"And we thought you weren't interested," replied Kiri.

"Not uninterested, just careful. I'm always interested in you and your Mom's safety," answered Lanny.

Maud, Agatha and Hettie all began talking at once.

"Is it true that Tom and Robert killed someone?"

"They surely fooled us."

"I guess we're just three foolish old women."

I went over to them and said, "You couldn't have known. They'd read articles about The Pauline Epistle and decided to see if they could make that work for them in getting hold of the church property. They laid an elaborate plan to blame you for the mischief they might do, covering up their real plan to somehow get the land around the church. They had a real estate developer all lined up. With the church property and the land that you'd signed over to them, they expected to turn a profit of over $4,000,000.

"But how did they know that we had the deed . . ."

"Or thought we did," said Maud.

". . . and the key and such?" asked Agatha.

"Sakes alive, Aggie, I believer I can answer that," responded Maud. "We told them! Do you remember those two nice young men this last summer that came to ask if they could sleep in the church picnic grove?"

"Land sakes, I do remember," added Nettie. "We had ourselves a picnic lunch with them and I remember telling them about dear Rev. Peterson and how much we missed the church and all the lovely times we had an, oh my . . ." she let her words fade into the air as realization dawned on her.

"But those young men had beards and long hair," Hettie protested, a bit weakly.

"Those boys stayed long enough to learn all about you then they left for awhile, is that right?" I asked.

"We thought they'd gone when low and behold a few months later Tom and Robert . . ."

"Clean-shaven and business-like?" asked Marie.

". . . Came and we let them stay in the church basement," finished Hettie.

"I remember now," recalled Maud. "That's when they began talking about the New Resurrection Church and Resort."

"We didn't quite understand the part about a resort," added Agatha.

"I thought they were going to sponsor camp meetings and revivals."

"That's also when they began to talk to us about you, Pip. I mean Rev. Franzen-whatever. How we should be against women preachers and how Rev. Peterson would want us to raise up against that new Bible-book, the Pauline Episcal, or something or other," explained Hettie.

"Epistle," corrected Marie. "It means 'letter.'"

"Yes, well we never really understood that, either," continued Hettie.

"Land sakes but we've been foolish," lamented Maud.

"And for our foolishness one person was killed," said Agatha sadly.

"And we might all have been incinerated," muttered Karl.

"You didn't force Tom and Robert to commit their crimes," said Marie. "They are guilty of their own greed."

"If it hadn't been you, it would have been someone else," said Kiri.

"Those two were out looking for trouble," added Sarah.

"None the less, if it hadn't been for you, we would have been in a terrible fix. I thank you," said Maud, quietly.

Agatha and Hettie voiced their agreement.

Maud paused for a moment and walked over to me. She looked perplexed.

"I do wonder something, however," she said. "How in the world did you happen to have a key to the church?"

"And how do you know so much out our church's history?" asked Hettie.

"Yeah, Mom, what about the key and all the other stuff? How come you know these things?" This from Sarah. "You told us a little before. Tell us more, now."

"As you know, I'm on special leave of absence from an appointment to a local church. But I'm still a member of Annual Conference so am expected to carry my fair share of Conference responsibilities. As such, I happen to chair an ad hoc committee to determine the future of the Bostwick Church and grounds. It seems that the Conference sort of dropped the ball on this one and has been trying to decide how to use or sell or dispose of this property for several years now. I was assigned to investigate and make a recommendation as to its use or disposal."

"You mean you're the one who will decide what happens here?" Kiri quickly got to the point.

"It's ironic, isn't it?" said Sarah.

"The decision won't be mine by myself, but yes, I would imagine my recommendations will carry some weight."

"And that recommendation would be . . ." Marie asked.

"I think this would be a wonderful place for a camp-group meeting place. It could be open in the summer for church groups and family reunions and such," I replied. "The problem with that is what else, finances. I just don't see the Conference being able to manage the cost of doing this well."

"Well, my dear," supplied Maud. I think we can help along those lines."

"Yes, and perhaps re-pay a debt long over-due," added Agatha.

"We would like to give our land to the Conference. That way they could sell it and have a trust fund. . ."

"A real trust fund this time," added Hettie.

". . . To care for the cost and upkeep of the church and grounds," continued Maud.

"Do you think you could arrange that?" queried Agatha, hopefully. "Our land is mostly woods and lake shore, would that be sellable?"

"And perhaps we could live in our little home for the rest of our lives," asked Maud. "I know I'd like that."

"But we could come over to some of the picnics and hymn sings and worship services, couldn't we?" she asked.

"If you wouldn't mind that some of them are led by women ministers," said Lanny, ever the realist.

"Oh my no," asserted Agatha. "We quite like women pastors now."

"Yes, they're so comforting and caring," said Hettie.

"And quite authoritative," added Marie.

"What, dear?" asked Maud.

"Wouldn't it be great to start things off with one big ice cream social and hymn sing?" Sarah's eyes lit up. "I love ice cream!"

Maud and Hettie and Agatha were still smiling as we drove out the driveway toward home.

Chapter Twenty-Three

The fireplace is blazing and a gentle snow is falling. Kiri and Sarah have both arrived safely home for Christmas. We'll decorate the Christmas tree later this evening. Lanny will help put it up. Kiri does the lights and then we girls decorate the tree as we listen to Christmas CD's and re-tell the stories of all the various ornaments.

The Pauline Epistle has been published. Yes, there were some very disgruntled conservative Christians who were upset but we seem to have weathered the heaviest part of that storm.

Tomorrow Marie and Pudge will be here to celebrate Christmas with us. We plan to take a drive to the Bostwick Church to have an evening of Christmas carols, readings, memories and fellowship. We've been assured that there will be homemade Christmas cookies, that there will be gifts under the tree, that we will be asked to recite our Christmas pieces and that we will sing our favorite carols. We will hear the Christmas story read from the Gospel of Luke one more time. There will be fresh pine boughs, holly, ivy and candles.

Church members from long ago and their families will be there to help celebrate. The Conference Committee on Camping will be represented.

I have been asked to preach from Rev. Peterson's pulpit.

Hettie, Maud and Agatha have cleaned the church until it's spotless.

Marie will play the organ. Kiri will sing O Holy Night. Sarah will read the story from Luke.

We are grateful for our places in the church. We will celebrate and give thanks for all God's mercies and grace.

Dedicated to my daughter

Sarah

and all the stories that are hers.

The Sisters of Sarah

❁ Chapter One ❁

The plane circled low over the Bosphorus River as it made its final landing approach.

Istanbul! It was like coming home after three years of being away. In the blink of an eye I remembered my first trip here ten years ago. I was visiting my daughter Sarah who had been attending the University of Marmara as an exchange student from Beloit College. We'd spent two weeks seeing the sights and visiting with her friends. That was when I became enthralled with the Hagia Sophia – the Church of the Holy Wisdom, built by Emperor Justinian in 635 A.D. It became a mosque during the Ottoman Empire and is now a Turkish National Museum. I remember Sarah's friend and classmate, Ali Ahmet, asking me what I felt as I stood in that beautiful place of worship, both for Christians and Muslims, of so many years ago.

"I can feel the presence, Christian and Muslim, of all those pious souls – and their prayers – I am surrounded by their prayers," I replied.

Again, seven years ago, followed by six years, five years, and four years ago, I'd returned to teach a series of enrichment classes at the University. I'd spent a month on these four separate occasions teaching mini-classes on American theatre and American idiom and culture. It was during these experiences that we began our "great experiment."

On two afternoons during the week along with several of my friends and students we'd go to the Hagia Sophia where we would sit and exchange dreams and ideas with any of the students who were so inclined.

We had some general rules:

- We were to listen politely to another's ideas;
- We were not to raise our voices in anger.

Our purpose was to find common ground. We were determined to share ideas, religious truths and cultural differences. We were determined to create and maintain friendship and understanding. Were we a bit naïve? Yes, I suppose we were. But it worked! We called ourselves the Wisdom Experience, basically because we met in the Hagia Sophia – the Church of the Holy Wisdom.

Much to our surprise and amazement WE grew and by the last time I was in Istanbul we numbered over five hundred people, mostly students and their friends. Those were glorious days and I still communicate with many of my original WE friends.

And now, from such humble beginnings, WE will expand and attempt to address itself to the world. The first ever international Wisdom Experience Conference will be held at the Hagia Sophia in Istanbul.

This WE, however, has become more mature, more organized and more worldly. Will it bear the stress of such change, I wonder.

"Please be sure to take all your belongings with you as you depart the plane," broke into my pleasant revelry. I gathered my purse and carry-on bag and made my way to the exit.

After all the official stamping and checking, I was ready to call a cab to take me to the University where I would be staying in the Guest House. I heard him first, and then saw him.

"Pip, do you remember me? How are you?" he asked in his oh so familiar voice.

My friend, Ali Ahmet, stood at the gate to greet me.

"You see," he said, "I'm not a simit seller!"

"I know," I responded, as I gave him a big hug. "After all, you're the reason I'm here!"

I must explain. Ali Ahmet was a friend of my daughter Sarah while she was here. A classmate, really. He later spent time with us in the USA so he could get work experience in an American bank. Ali Ahmet was like a son to us. And, although we always kidded that he would become a simet seller (a peddler on the streets selling simit-bread), he had recently become the youngest national official in Turkey. He was the Minister of Finance and was already responsible for many changes in the Turkish fiscal system. I hadn't expected that he would be able to get away from his office to meet my plane.

We gathered my bags from the luggage carousel and went to the car. We chatted happily, renewing our friendship and remembering old times and old friends.

Anna has gone on to school in London as she hoped.

Zia is a doctor working in Ankara.

Chadra is married to a professor and they have two children, and so on.

"And you, Ali, what's new and exciting with you?" I asked.

He blushed and smiled.

"OK, what's her name?" I guessed.

"She is from the United States. – a doctor and she has been working with the University to set up classes in her specialty, pediatric surgery. She is wonderfully gifted, I'm so proud of her . . ."

"And her name is . . .?"

"She's from the Midwest, too, like you are. She comes from South Dakota, can you imagine! Her father is a minister and her mother is a nurse . . ."

"And her name, Ali, her name . . ."

"Oh, it's LeeAnn Nelson. Imagine, Pip, she's Norwegian like you!"

He was right! Although my paternal roots are deeply German, my mother's family came from Norway. And, although we didn't eat lutefisk (we all said we were too German for that) we did relish yulekaake, sandbackles and all the other wonderful Norwegian treats.

"She even tried to get me to eat Norwegian rice! Imagine that! She was very surprised when I said I'd already had it. That Christmas I was living with you. Remember!? She wants to meet you," Ali continued.

We talked of friends and plans for the Wisdom Experience scheduled in one week's time. In no time at all we arrived at the Guest House on the campus of the University of Marmara. I would be staying there, in a small efficiency apartment where I had stayed during my earlier visits. I was greeted at the desk by my old friend Anna.

"Oh, Dr. Pip, it is so good to have you return to us. You will be in suite number forty-three, your old suite, yes? Let me give you your keys."

All through the lobby I was greeted with smiles and "Mehrhaba." I took one of the elevators to the fourth four and quickly went to my suite.

"Suite" is an operative word for a large room divided into living areas. I did have my own little kitchen and bathroom, however, and was delighted to be back into my own cozy home away from home.

Ali helped with the luggage.

"And is Lanny going to be here?" he asked.

"Yes, he'll arrive on the last day of the conference and then we'll play tourists for a while," I answered.

"Maybe I can take him to a game," Ali said. "My home team plays about then."

While Ali lived with us, he and Lanny had an almost father-son relationship. I could see them both together cheering on their team. (Lanny is a die-hard Green Bay Packers fan. Ali became one, too.) Of course, it wasn't the Packers, but it would be the Turkish equivalent.

"I've got to get back to my office," Ali said. "We'll go out to eat this evening, right?"

"Sounds good," I answered. "I've got a few last minute plans to work on and then it will be nap time for me."

"See you about 7:00 p.m., Pip," he said, and left.

I was glad to have time for myself. I called Lanny, did some unpacking, took a shower and lay down to take a nap.

❂ Chapter Two ❂

The next few days went by in a blur of activity. We were expecting Conference attendees from twenty different countries. Since English was the business language of most of those attending, it was to be the spoken and written language of the Conference. The planning committee had arranged for several interpreters to be available, however. Hopefully, we had everything covered.

We had five different committees that had been busy planning and making preparations for well over six months, some having met for more than a year. The larger planning committee met several times to be sure all the preparations were completed or, at least, anticipated. Excitement amongst the committee members was very evident. We met one last time before the opening of the WE Conference.

"We have five hundred and fifty registrants as of two days ago," reported the registrar, Mohammed Musa. "All of those have been confirmed at hotels or guest houses. We will have shuttles to meet the various arrivals at the airport."

"Our opening reception is scheduled for 8:00 p.m. on Monday evening. We will be meeting at the Hagia Sophia for instructions, a brief welcoming ceremony," and so forth.

"The first of the major sessions begins at 10:00 a.m. on Tuesday morning," and so on, as all the pieces fell in place for what promised to be a wonderful four-day celebration of world community and openness. Our speakers would be thought provoking and challenging, the panel discussions were interesting and there would be much time for fellowship, conversation and getting to know one another. Oh yes, our theme, ONE GOD: Many Names has raised eyebrows among some in various religious communities. Yet there are many who are anxious to see the success of our conference. As one of my colleagues said to me, "Pip, it's time, it's past time."

After spending time going over details, fine-tuning plans and making sure we were all on the 'same page,' we adjourned.

Fajed Almir, our financial manager, came over to me and said, "Pip, I'm so pleased with all the planning and arrangements. Both my wife and I and our four children will be attending. I am also bringing my brother and some of his family. He is an imam in Ankara." He shook my hand and left, saying he would see me soon.

I gathered all my notes and papers together, keeping the "still to be done" list on the top.

After a quick lunch at a little sidewalk café I quickly made my way to the little grocery store closest to my apartment. I picked up lots of fresh fruit and vegetables and other assorted goodies to keep me from starving. After a bus ride home I returned to my little apartment and put my groceries away.

Several of the planning committee members were also staying at the Guest House and I thought it might be a good idea to know what rooms they were in. Anna was at the desk so I asked for the room numbers. She wrote their names and numbers on a slip of paper and gave them to me.

Jack Trevor Anderson is professor of New Testament Culture at Yale. I knew him from the time I'd done one semester on a dig in Turkey when completing my PhD. Jack is here with his wife, Carolyn. They are in room 631.

Karl Riddlington is a New Testament scholar and author of Christianity and Islam: God and Allah. He is retired but had been on the faculty of Wesley Seminary when I was a student there. His wife, Hannah, is also here with him. They are in room 529.

I decided to buzz them and see if they would be interested in dessert in my apartment tonight about 8:00 p.m. They said they would be delighted so I hurried back to my apartment to make the dessert for later.

I was busily blending the ingredients for the 'caramel crème' when the phone rang. It was Ali asking how I was. He thought maybe I'd like to meet his friend, LeeAnn. Since I knew that Ali loved caramel flavored anything (we'd introduced him to caramel when he lived with us when he was in the US) and I, of course, wanted to meet LeeAnn, I said, "yes, why don't you come for dessert about 8:00 p.m. Better still, come a little early, about 7:00 p.m., and we'll have a chance to talk. LeeAnn and I will be able to get acquainted before the other guests arrive."

"That sounds wonderful, Pip. We'll see you then," replied Ali.

ISTANBUL, 1525 C.E.

I have found safety! It has been six months since the fire that destroyed my home and killed my family. The sisters have chosen me to be the chronicler of our group. I have decided to begin with my story.

It began simply enough. My father was the business man of accounts for a wealthy member of our small community. My family lived well but frugally. There were six of us; my father, Simeon; my mother, Martha; my two oldest brothers, Caleb and Andrew; myself, Sarah, and my baby brother, Joseph. We were kept busy with our small farm and, of course, father's work with Casca's business affairs.

One night when my father came home he called us together and told us to gather our belongings. We were going to leave before dawn. We must hurry.

"But the farm, father, who will care for the farm?" asked Caleb.

"We will stay and care for the animals," said Andrew. "We are not afraid, father."

"You do not understand, my son," responded our father. "I have seen and heard too much. Casca has betrayed our community." And then he explained about hearing a conversation earlier today. "I thought no one knew I heard but Ezra passed me a note to warn me. They will come to take me away tomorrow. They will send you two into the military and I fear what they will do to my dear wife and our lovely Sarah. I cannot risk remaining here. These are ruthless men who have much to loose if I should make known what I heard. Now come quickly, we must hurry."

The rest of the night was spent packing food enough and household goods so we might leave. Father instructed me to go into his shelf and get his household funds.

"And Sarah, be prepared to dress as your brothers. They will not expect that."

We planned to leave before dawn.

We hitched oxen to a two-wheeled cart for Mamma and baby Joseph. Papa felt if we could get as far as Smyrna we might seek refuge with Christian friends there.

Then it happened. Horses and riders rode into our enclosure throwing spears and flaming, oil-soaked torches. They smashed everything they could. My father tried to protect my mother and Joseph. Caleb and Andrew were killed trying to save the livestock.

I ran into the house hoping to help Papa. Both he and mama shoved me into the root cellar and covered it with rugs. I stayed there, cowering for what seemed like hours. I finally fell asleep. When I awoke all was quiet. I carefully slid open the trap door. As I did I could hear two men talking. They could not see me because I was hidden behind a pile of smoldering debris.

"Is that all of them?" asked one.

"Yes, the two in the yard died hard but I have see to it – they are dead. The old man, his wife and baby son were in the house. No one could have survived the fire."

"What of the young woman?" asked the other man. "She is the one Casca wanted."

"She ran into the house. She did not come out. As you can see," gesturing to the smoking heap that had been my house, "no one could have lived through that inferno." They laughed, nodded and walked away. "Too bad about the girl, though. She'd have brought a good price. Casca won't be happy."

"When is Casca ever happy," was the last I heard of them.

I waited all day to be sure it was safe to come out. Some neighbors came by to gawk and scavenge what they could from what was left. One took the three or four chickens who had managed to survive. One took my mother's brass pots. I know I couldn't trust any of them to help me.

As night fell I rose from my hiding place. I was dirty and my clothes were torn. I went to the cattle shed where I knew my brothers kept extra clothes. I bathed and washed my hair in the cattle trough. After putting on my brother, Caleb's, clothes and sandals I was able to pack a shoulder bag with food and water. Andrew had left a knife in the stall and with it I cut my hair off. There, I thought, I am now a young man.

I went back to my safe hiding place and found my father's bag of coins. I put it, along with Andrew's knife, in my leather pack.

Although I did not know the right words, I stood and prayed at the gap in the wall which would be my exit. Fearing that I would not be able to pull myself away from here if I looked again at their bodies, I quietly slipped out of the enclosure. I began to walk swiftly toward Smyrna.

"May God bless my feet and keep my heart strong" was my prayer. In between my sobs and tears I vowed I would escape from here and that I would be strong.

"I will be strong and remember Papa and Mama, and Caleb and Andrew and my dear little Joseph. And God accept them into your heavenly kingdom."

I walked and ran at night and tried to stay hidden during the days. I continued this way for two weeks when I ran out of food. I was able to go into small market towns and replenish my stores. I knew I was getting closer to Istanbul. I decided to go there, out of curiosity, mostly. After all, I was fourteen, alive and on my own.

A young girl alone would have been very noticeable so I kept the disguise of my brother's clothes. I walked through the gates of the city about noon. There were streets and shops and so many people. I'd never seen so many people before. And they all seemed to be in a rush to get somewhere. I managed to find my way to an open market where I bought olives and nuts and fresh fruit to eat. I walked through the busy streets and found myself in front of a huge and beautiful domed building. There were tall minarets. Then I heard a loud voice calling people to prayer. That seemed like a good idea so I entered the building to say my prayers for my family. I was pushed and shoved so hard that I lost my balance. I crawled to get out of the crowd and found a quiet place to sit. As I sat leaning against a wall in the corner, a woman came up to me and put her arms around my shoulder.

"Come with me, dear," she whispered.

I didn't know why I should but I trusted her. She led the way out of the building and away from the crowd.

"Sit here, my dear," she spoke softly to me. "We'll wait until it's less crowded and safe."

"But how did you know . . ." I protested.

"It isn't hard. There are so many of you. But come, I'll take you someplace safe."

She took my arm and led me to the large mosque (I later learned called the Hagia Sophia, also known as the Church of Holy Wisdom).

She took me around carts and market booths and what looked to be a cemetery until we were away from the crowd and alone. Then she led me to one of the corners of the building, by the great foundation and, after checking to see no one watched, we somehow managed to go through a small doorway, down some dark, steep steps and into a small room, illumined only by one small oil lamp.

She gestured to the one chair in the room and said, "sit and wait here. I won't be long," and disappeared into the darkness.

❁ Chapter Three ❁

It was a wonderful evening! Ali brought LeeAnn about 7:00 p.m. and we had an opportunity to become acquainted. She was a tall, slim, blond woman who looked younger than her thirty years. Ali is obviously very taken with her and, I believe, she with him. And yes, she is, indeed from South Dakota!

"Where did you do your undergraduate work?" I asked.

"Oh, it's a small liberal arts college. You've probably never heard of it. It's called Dakota Wesleyan University and it is in Mitchell, South Dakota.

"Really?" I answered gleefully, and began to sing the first phrase of The Scotchman, the Dakota Wesleyan school hymn,

> "Show me the Scotchman
> who doesn't love the thistle?"

And LeeAnn chimed in,

> "Show me the Englishman
> who doesn't love the rose?
> Show me the true hearted one
> of old Wesleyan who doesn't
> love the spot where the
> tumbleweed grows."

We laughed and hugged, and laughed some more. Ali stood with a puzzled look on his face.

"Oh Ali, you look so surprised!" exclaimed LeeAnn.

"We went to the same college! Can you believe that?" I said. "It really is a small world!"

LeeAnn and I exchanged memories of our years at D.W.U. Amazingly we even knew some of the same people.

By the time our other guests arrived, we were fast friends. I almost had the feeling that Ali felt a little left out.

Karl and Hannah, Jack and Carolyn arrived together. It wasn't long before we were talking about our families, our jobs and about the tourist spots we had seen since arriving in Istanbul. As our conversation began to wind down, LeeAnn asked, "How did you happen to select your topic, 'ONE GOD: Many Names?' Won't that be considered heresy by some?"

Jack answered that, "Yes, it is probably controversial to some folks but it is surely an appropriate theme to discuss in this age of separation and mistrust."

A lively discussion ensued as each of us added our thoughts on the subject.

"It seems to me that the theological issues surrounding Christianity, Islam and Judaism drive the political issues in which we are deeply inured. We really need to talk about our beliefs and how they impact the way we live," concluded Karl.

"I believe that to be true," responded Ali. "The problem is that you, how do you say it; wade into pretty deep and dark waters. I hope you have taken some caution for your safety."

Yes, we'd thought of it and we had a very basic plan for security in place.

"It's not terribly sophisticated," I explained. "I vacillate between hoping and believing nothing untoward will happen and examining and re-examining our security measures. We have a team of thirty people who are led by one security professional. We've also alerted and connected with the police department here in Istanbul. They have been very cooperative and gracious. Hopefully that will be enough."

Hannah stood up. "I've got to meet with my committee early tomorrow morning to go over last minute details. Who would have thought that coffee and cookies would be so complicated!" (Hannah is the chair of hospitality for this conference.) As the others rose and went to the door we said our good-byes and they all went to their rooms for the night. I quickly did the few dishes that were there. As

I was getting ready for bed there was a knock at the door. I looked through the peephole.

"Ali! Come in!"

"I won't stay long. I want to remind you to be careful, Pip. Not everyone is as open-minded as those on your committee. Just be careful," and with that, he left.

I locked the door and went to bed. Tomorrow we were going to do a walk-through of the Sophia and then we would be ready for the five hundred plus registrants in the afternoon. I played scenario after scenario over in my mind as I lay in the dark. Sleep finally came. Dreams came as well.

ISTANBUL, 1525 C.E.

I waited for what seemed hours. As I sat in the darkness I turned over in my mind the events of the past few weeks. None of it made sense to me. Who would want to kill my family? Why? And where was I now? Should I flee? But which way was out? The oil lamp flickered and sent a small beam of light across the room. There were no windows. Just as I was about to get up and leave the woman came for me.

"Come with me, my dear," she repeated her earlier request. "You are safe. No one here will harm you," and she led me through a small archway to some more steps downward. I followed cautiously. We walked for perhaps twenty feet, still travelling downward, when we came to a hinged, wooded door. We entered a well-lit room which had a large table, several chairs, rugs, cushions and curtains. The woman who led me (I later learned her name is Elizabeth) indicated I should sit.

I was terrified! There were several veiled women in the room and they stood back and appeared to watch me.

"Welcome, my dear," the well-dressed woman at the head of the table spoke to me, asking me about my family, my life and how I came to be in Istanbul.

"Yes, we had heard of the massacre in Lyconos of Simeon's family. Martha was especially dear to us. This is where she met Simeon. And now, in the midst of your sadness and turmoil, God has brought you here to us. Welcome, our dear Simeon and Martha's daughter. Welcome our dear Sarah.

I stayed in this place where I was fed, clothed, cared for and made to feel welcome. I met many women, some who stayed and many others who came and went.

I was taught many new things. I learned languages, cultures and even ethnic foods from many places! Eventually I was entrusted with the secret of The Sisters of Sarah.

Chapter Four

Actually I had been somewhat cavalier in speaking of the security arrangements. We did, indeed, have a security team led by one highly trained professional and made up of thirty volunteers. The volunteers, however, were all members of various branches of the armed forces security teams. We had American, Turkish, British, Canadian and Israeli troops working together. (Quite frankly, I considered the make-up and cooperation of this team to be one of our major accomplishments!) They had been meeting for two weeks prior to the conference setting in place highly technical surveillance equipment. They had been in conversation with each other and shared ideas and technology.

Everyone who entered the Hagia Sophia or was registered for this conference would be photographed and placed under some surveillance. There are only a very few of us who are aware of this tight security. I appreciated Ali's concern that I be careful. There had been rumors of unrest among some of the more conservative brothers and sisters in each of the respective faith communities.

ISTANBUL, 1525 C.E.

"The Sisters of Sarah!" I exclaimed. "But my name is Sarah!"

"Yes, dear, you have surely been sent to us," responded Elizabeth. "Come along, there is much to learn. You must return to your lessons."

Reader, I cannot write everything that has been my experience since coming to Sophia but I now am allowed to put in writing some things.

The Sisters of Sarah are an ancient secret society of women, Jewish, Muslim and Christian. We work for the safety and encouragement and advancement of all women.

We seek out, find, and have brought to us, through our far-reaching network of sisters, women who have been abused, beaten and abandoned by society, their fathers and husbands. We operate in Istanbul out of a secret warren of tunnels and rooms placed under Hagia Sophia by Emperor Justinian for purposes of his own. After his death, some fifty years later, one of the original workmen's daughters named Sarah remembered her father telling of such a secret place. It is a long story. Sometime later she and a group of friends sought it out and formed the Sisters of Sarah in honor of Abraham's wife, Sarah. If Abraham is considered the father of monotheism, hence the cousin faiths of Judaism, Christianity and Islam, then Sarah is truly our mother, our sister and our common link.

Since that time until now (I write this in the summer of 1525) the sisterhood has existed caring for women of all faiths and many with none.

I have been deemed able to become a teacher and scribe for our group. Others garden, craft beautiful arts, sew, knit or paint. Yet others become doctors, teachers, counselors, theologians and nurses. Each has a place in our organization.

We are a diverse group including all ages, cultures and backgrounds. Many are able to live with their families in their own homes. Others have only the Sophia as home. Some earn money by their skills. And, I was surprised to learn, others are wealthy patrician matrons who willingly share what they have so all may be safe, well, educated and fed. We all have tasks. Elizabeth is our "eye." She finds and brings young women of need to us. Just as she found me.

Daily I grow stronger and wiser. I am learning to read and write Hebrew and Arabic. I also am learning the history and theology of our faiths. I continue to read and write Greek and have learned some Latin. It is good to be a part of a family. But oh, Mama and Papa, I still miss you so.

❁ Chapter Five ❁

The day dawned bright and clear. I gathered all the papers and reports I had been working on and placed them in my brief case.

I was humming as I took my shower and got dressed. After checking again to see if I had what I needed for the day, I went downstairs to the dining room for breakfast. By now friends had gathered and we sat around tables eating the typical Turkish breakfast of hard boiled eggs, olives, tomatoes, farmer cheese and warm, crusty bread. And Chia, always hot and plentiful.

Jack and Carolyn were ready to go so we shared a taxi. Karl and Hannah would meet with her hospitality committee.

The Hagia Sophia is imposing at any time. Early morning is no exception. Already it was surrounded by the hustle and bustle of the various participants of the conference as well as the usual tourists, visitors and staff.

I stepped out of the cab following Jack and Carolyn.

"Are you coming?" asked Carolyn.

"Yes, go ahead," I said. "I just want to soak it all up. I love these grounds. I can sense the presence of all those souls who've come here. I may be silly but I think they would approve of what we're doing. Besides, I don't really need to be anywhere until this afternoon."

Carolyn nodded and she and Jack walked into the 'Sophia' ready for their jobs as registrars and later, Jack as discussion leader.

I wandered amongst the monuments, markers and tombstones around the grounds.

"Doctor Pip," I heard from behind one of the larger monuments.

"Majed!" I exclaimed. "How are you today?"

Majed was a friend from my earlier visits to Istanbul. He is an inspector in the Istanbul Metropolitan Police and assigned to the conference.

"I am fine. I like to be familiar with my assignments," he said. "If you need me for anything, I'll be here," he indicated the grounds around the Sophia, "you have but to call me." He hesitated, and then, "as a matter of fact, I'd like to give you this." He handed me a device that looked like a very small cell phone.

"It's actually something that I have put together. Keep it on your person and if you need me for anything you have but to call my name. I will hear you. It will also give me your location. Take it, please, Dr. Pip. I will feel better if you have it. Even though you probably won't need it."

I put it in the zipper side pocket of my purse.

"Why are you so concerned that I have this?" I asked, turning to face him, but he was gone. I laughed to myself. Majed was the perfect "under-cover" man. He was there but he wasn't. He came but no one ever saw him.

I continued to walk around the side of the Hagia Sophia. The ground was rough so I was watching where I put my feet. As I looked down I noticed what appeared to be roughly carved letters in the recessed archway of the foundation. I looked closer. Surely these were letters carved into the stone. Written many years ago, carved in what looked to be Greek, Arabic and Hebrew. My curiosity was peaked. I'd have to ask someone.

ISTANBUL, 1527 C.E.

Two years have passed since I came to Istanbul. In that time I have been well educated in Latin, Greek, Arabic and Hebrew. I speak French and English as well and am able to move about in Istanbul society easily. I have become part of the inner council of The Sisters of Sarah and have travelled across the length of the Ottoman Empire working for the Sisters as I travel. Next year I am planning to marry a very nice, well-to-do young man from near Rome. I have met him twice and we get along very well. His name is Antonio Gaius. He and his family run a trading company. He is Christian and we both look forward to our marriage.

For now I am teaching a younger woman to become a scribe and chronicler of the sisterhood. She was whipped and beaten by her brothers after her parents died. Then she was left in the gutter to die. Our good sister, Elizabeth, found her and brought her to us. She has chosen to change her name from Olympas to Sarah. Another sister of Sarah!

Chapter Six

Sarah! That's what the engraved letters in the wall spell out! I was right, they are in Hebrew, Arabic and Greek, says my colleague Aristotle ben Joshua, professor of Antiquities at the Hebrew Institute in Athens.

"See here, Pip," he explained, as he took a rubbing of the letters, "the chisel slipped a bit and left a mark. But these are surely the name of Sarah in the three languages you thought. Interesting that they should be here with no other indication why."

Why would the name Sarah be carved into a somewhat hidden alcove at the back foundation of the Hagia Sophia? A mystery, certainly. I just love mysteries!

I walked around the foundations and into the Sophia where I was met with much hustle and excitement. People had begun to gather. Old friends greeted one another and strangers were introduced as each stood in line to register. A feeling of anticipation hovered in the air. There seemed to be so much hope that somehow if we would just come together and talk, we might begin the journey of understanding.

"Hello, Pip," I heard to my left. "I'm glad to see you again." It was LeeAnn.

"Hi! I'm a bit surprised to see you," I responded.

She laughed and said, "I was so intrigued by the idea of this conference that I begged and, yes, nagged Ali to bring me. Technically he signed me up as an emergency first aid person, which, of course, I'm happy to do. In reality, I was just so curious I couldn't stay away. I hope you don't mind."

"Of course not. I'm delighted you're here. Come with me and let me introduce you to some more of the participants."

LeeAnn and I moved through the crowds as I introduced her to many of the visitors.

We had arranged to have luncheon served to the members of the committees and I invited LeeAnn to share it with us.

"Ali is here somewhere. I think we're going out . . . oh, there he is." "Ali! Here I am," as she waved and gestured toward him.

Ali made his way through the crowd and hugged both LeeAnn and me.

"How has your day been so far, Pip?" he asked. "I know you've waited a long time for this event."

I told him about 'Sarah' chiseled on the wall.

"You mean like 'Sarah was here?'" he joked.

"If that's what it was whoever did it was a pretty good graffiti artist. It looks old – as if it's been there for a thousand years."

We talked as we walked toward the front entrance where Ali had a car waiting.

"You're welcome to come with us," he said. "We're going to have Iscandar."

Mmmm, one of my favorite meals in Turkey. "I'd love to but I have to meet with some people, last minute details, you know."

Ali and LeeAnn drove off and I re-entered the Sophia only to be immediately inundated with details –

"Here's the preliminary count . . ."

"What should I do about this one . . .?"

"We've had more registrations than we expected . . ."

and

"Good news, the cookies were a hit!" (Laughter)

"Here's the final schedule for this afternoon . . ." and, at last,

"Let's go to lunch." (That was by me, by the way. I was famished!)

Lunch was served under large tent-like awnings in the space between the Hagia Sophia and the Blue Mosque. We were served buffet-style and seated around tables of six. Our menu was light, refreshing and tasty; fresh melons, strawberries, cheeses, cold slices of chicken or lamb, tomatoes, olives and yogurt. Chia or lemonade was available to drink. Most of the servers were students from the University. Several came up to me and introduced themselves as children or younger siblings of students I had known when I taught here.

One introduced herself as Sophia, "you know, for the Hagia Sophia. My mom and dad used to come and listen and talk with you. They brought me with them. You would pick me up and talk with me. I remember a song you taught me."

"Yes, you're Almed and Safra's daughter. I remember you well," I responded. "It's wonderful to see you." And we sang the 'Sandman' song my mother taught me.

"I want to tell you something, Dr. Pip. "I heard some people talking. They were mingling with other conference people. They didn't think the conference was wonderful at all. I'm afraid for you, Dr. Pip. Please be careful. They were dressed like Arab Muslims but they sounded American to me." And with that she was gone.

Good grief, not another warning! I was beginning to feel a little paranoid. How could there be such darkness and hate in such a beautiful place?

As I walked back toward the Sophia I called Ed Arnold. Ed is in charge of security for the conference. I asked him if we could meet. I needed some reassurance, for sure.

"Right, Pip. I'll be at the registration tables in about five minutes. See you there."

When I arrived at the tables, Ed was already there. I shared with him all the warnings and cautions and ended by telling him Sophia's comments.

"We'll watch for anything funny, of course. But we can't just frisk people who look Muslim."

We talked for a few minutes more and then his cell phone buzzed. "I've got to get this. See you. And quit worrying!"

"Thanks, Ed," and got up and went to the table where Jack and Carolyn were sitting.

"Everything OK here?" I asked.

They nodded enthusiastically. "It's been exciting to meet people from different places," said Carolyn. "Just look at some of these," as she showed me some of the registration forms. There were people from all over the world; Muslim, Jew and Christian. "We even have a party of six Buddhist monks. They said they were here to observe and to 'cheer us on' and 'lend support.' Oh, and look. Many are professors and clergy but not everyone. Here's one mother and daughter who came to support women's rights. And here's a couple from New Mexico. He's Catholic and she's Jewish. They said if they can get along its high time we all did." Clearly Carolyn was already enjoying the conference.

ISTANBUL, 1563 C.E.

After so many years I have returned. My beloved Antonio has been dead almost a year. I have returned to work with the sisterhood once more.

Antonio and I talked of this often. Let me explain.

Antonio and I were married for thirty-five wonderful years. We have five children; Simeon, Joseph, Caleb, Andrew and Martha. They are grown now, with children of their own. Simeon and his wife, Maria, run the Gaius family business. They have three dear children. Joseph is a sea captain and his cargo is brought first to the Gaius warehouses. His wife and baby died in childbirth. Caleb is our professor. He teaches theology at Padua. His wife, Athene, is an artisan and creates beautiful tapestries. They have two boys, Antonio and Marcellus. Andrew is a physician and works in small villages outside of Rome. Angelina, his wife, is a nurse. They have three children; Luke, Paul and Miriam. And Martha, our baby, is our firebrand. She lives with Joseph (perhaps that is why he is at sea so much of the time) and vows to never marry and become any man's property! "But Marti," I say, "I was never treated as such by your Papa."

"Yes, but Papa was different. I will not let anyone rule me." And so it goes.

Pardon my wandering pen. It is the fault of a very proud mama.

As it came closer to Antonio's death, we spoke of what I would do.

"Go back, my Sarah. Go back to Sophia. You can do much work there. You will have all the money you need. I have seen to that. Go, help your suffering sisters. If you need it, you have my blessings. Oh, and" as an after thought he added, "take Martha with you. It will do her good." I knew there was a twinkle in his eye when he said that.

Three short days later my Antonio went to be in Christo.

I left to go to Istanbul. Only my children know where I truly went. Others were told I was going to family in Smyrna.

Upon my return to the Sisters of Sarah, I was greeted and accepted back into the fold, almost as if I'd never left. Save for one difference. I was chosen to become Mother Sarah. I would have a council of advisors and together we would determine the direction of the sisterhood. I daily thank God for the family of Sarah, for my family and for the years I had with dear, sweet Antonio.

And yes, I did bring Martha with me. She has much to learn.

Chapter Seven

The first afternoon session went well. We introduced our speakers and leaders and shared a brief history of the Wisdom Experience.

I spoke of the theme, ONE GOD: Many Names and was pleased to receive an appreciative and warm response. We introduced Dr. Almir Mojed, head librarian at the Turkish Institute in Athens, Dr. Nathan Greenblatt, curator and librarian at the Hebrew Institute in Athens, and Dr. Carin Nelson-Anderson, theologian and head of mid-Eastern languages at Bergen Evangelical School for Theology. These three had put together a wonderfully rich book booth for our participants to peruse. It even included coffee, Chia, ice cream and an internet connection. They called it "Holy Not-So-Grounds."

We'd put together two or three different two-hour tours of Istanbul's finest "tourist" spots. They included the Blue Mosque, Sulimann's Mosque, the Cisterns, Topkapi and several other places of interest.

We announced these options and reminded people to return here for the 7:00 p.m. banquet and speech by Dr. Ibrahim el Maka, head of the Department of Theological Studies at the University of History and Culture in Cairo. Dr. el Maka has long been a voice in speaking out about our shared values, history and belief systems. It promises to be an interesting evening.

ISTANBUL, 1565 C.E.

The Sisters of Sarah is growing! We have expanded and placed various members in outposts around the world. We have S.O.S. houses in Rome, Venice, Baghdad and Paris and finally, this past week, we have received word that a building has been rented and furnished in London. It is on Bread Lane, very near to many houses of ill repute. I'm proud to say my beloved Martha is its matron.

Martha, with all her energy and wit has learned to focus and direct it to a cause which is greater than she. We will expect to hear good things from London.

I continue to work in Istanbul although I did take a brief hiatus to visit my home town of Lyconos, south of Smyrna. I travelled with three of the sisters. We had four drivers-guards who cared for us and our needs well.

Poor little Lyconos – there isn't much left of it. The place where my family lived has grown over and gone wild. I brought a small memorial plaque for my family with me. Hector, one of our drivers, placed it for me on the approximate place my parents died.

I understand that no one would buy it or build on it. It is reputed to be haunted. The large household of Casca is completely gone. He died two years after I left. In the end, no one would work for him. Ezra told several people in the community of Casca's fraudulent dealings and immoral trade in human life. Casca's secret chambers where he tortured slaves were discovered. He was left to die by himself.

Lyconos is now only a small bump on the road to Smyrna and Istanbul.

❁ Chapter Eight ❁

It was a beautiful starlit night in Istanbul. There was a balmy light breeze and the temperature was 72 degrees. Perfect!

The banqueting tents and tables were lighted by candles. The food was a wonderful collation of fresh vegetable salad, olives, cheese, sliced lamb, beef and chicken, apricots, strawberries, melon slices and yogurt. There were also tortes of chocolate, caramel and fruit. Of course, Chai, iced tea, coffee with Turkish delight and baklava.

As the meal was coming to a close, Ed Arnold gestured for me to talk with him.

"Pip, we've got our first real glitch," he said. "One of the guests has been kidnapped. They left a note addressed to you." He handed me a note, written in Arabic but translated into English.

"Pip Franzen –

This is just a sample –

Do not tamper with God's will –

Next time it will be you.

For Allah

"Who did they take?" I asked.

"A guest from the United States, young man by the name of Andrew Whitaker. He's a seminary student at Yale."

We talked about options. Both of us agreed to remain silent in order to avoid panic.

"I've got all my resources on this already," he said. "No one else need know about this, at least not yet. Whitaker didn't have a roommate. What we need to do now is watch you more carefully. If they could snatch you, it would very effectively end the conference."

Chapter Nine

As it happened, it was to be a very eventful night.

First of all, our speaker, Dr. el Maka, was an eloquent voice for our conference. He shared heartfelt thoughts of why and how we might come together as people of faith. I remember him saying, "In reality the blasphemy of our faith's today is believing that one is superior over another. If God is God is God, then we need to openly find many ways to worship and serve God. If Christ is how you experience God, then I encourage you to act all the more Christ-like. If God is heard from prophets or from the Qur'an, or in prayers, or in Law or tradition, listen to them. But be sure that God is, God creates and God loves. And God calls us to live in peace with one another."

I noticed amidst the applause there was a group of observers who were not very happy with what el Maka had said.

Do they have any connection to Andrew's disappearance? Oh dear, now I'm looking for trouble where there probably is none.

The second noteworthy event occurred after all the other festivities were over. It was about 1:15 a.m. The delegates had gone off to their hotel rooms and the clean up crew was gathering trash, putting chairs away and preparing for the morning sessions. I was about to head back to my apartment when my cell phone rang.

"Hello," I said wearily.

"Pip, Ed Arnold here. You won't believe this. We have our college student back! He's here with me now."

"Where are you? I asked.

"I'm at the registration area in the Sophia."

"I'll be right there," I answered, and began walking quickly to meet him.

It took me about five minutes to walk the distance, slowed down by having to avoid piles of chairs, tables and stacks of garbage bags.

"So tell me what's up," I said as I approached Ed.

"It was the strangest experience," answered a tall young man. His name tag identified him as Andrew Whitaker, Yale, U.S.A.

"I was grabbed from behind in the men's room. I was at Topkapi on the afternoon tour," he explained. "They must have used chloroform or something. I don't remember a thing."

"Let's go over here where we can be more comfortable," I suggested. I indicated a lounge-type area that my feet would welcome.

"It was like this," continued Andrew. "I signed up for the afternoon tour. It was really neat. I loved the Roman Cisterns. We'd been at Topkapi for awhile. I wandered away from our tour group to use the restroom."

"Did anyone seem to be following you or taking particular notice of you?" asked Ed.

"Not that I noticed. Oh, wait; there was this one funny looking guy. He was dressed, well, kind of what you'd expect a tourist to be wearing."

"And can you describe that?" asked Ed.

"He had a tee shirt on with a big logo on it. Some sports team I think. He was wearing a black and red baseball cap and he had a big camera case. I remember he bumped me with it. I felt a nudge and then a prick. It hurt and I rubbed my arm. It drew blood."

Ed nodded, all the while taking notes. "We'll want to get a blood sample from you, Andrew. That may be why you can't remember anything."

"You think they drugged me?" Andrew looked frightened.

"Go on, tell us what happened next," I encouraged.

"I can't remember what happened next. All I remember is finding myself in a dark, cave-like room with my hands and feet tied. I had some kind of tape across my mouth. I must have sat there for awhile. No one came. I was scared that I'd been left there to die. I was terrified."

Andrew began to tremble. He rubbed his wrists where he had been tied. "I don't remember seeing any kind of door; I thought I was sealed in. And I recall thinking that 'here I am going to die and I don't even know why!' I tried to pray, but ended up crying. I tried to take deep breaths. I tried to picture Jesus. I even hummed a bunch of hymns. Actually, the hymns helped a little. I must have fallen asleep. I remember I woke up and someone was talking to me in a foreign language. It was a woman and she was cutting the rope on my hands and feet. Before she took the tape off my mouth she said in English, 'You must be quiet. I am a friend and will get you out of here but you must make no noise.' After that she helped me stand up, took off the tape and took my hand saying, 'follow me quickly. They watch this passage every five minutes!' She pulled me along a dark passage until we came to a dead-end, a wall of huge stones and bricks. She tapped one of the stones on the wall. It must have been some sort of spring because it opened. We quickly went through and the wall closed behind us." He paused for a moment and both Ed and I looked at each other with a thousand questions on our faces.

"What happened next?" asked Ed.

"I'm a little fuzzy about all of this, but here goes," and taking a deep breath, Andrew continued.

"She said her name was Sarah. She told me we still needed to be quiet and then she whispered, 'You have nothing to fear from me. However, we must protect you from knowing certain things. I need to blindfold your eyes. I will hold your hand and lead you to safety.' I almost ran away but to tell you the truth, I was too scared, it was too dark and Sarah was too beautiful for words. She put a blindfold over my face and took my hand. We walked for about five minutes. Kind of like in circles sometimes. We walked up and down and stopped and turned. I lost track of which way and how many turns. Sometimes I thought I heard voices, like in another room. I could have sworn once or twice I felt a breeze or maybe like someone's breathe on me. Anyway, after awhile I thought we were outdoors and then we walked for awhile in another big circle. Then it felt like we were inside some building. I couldn't tell. Then Sarah leaned over and kissed my cheek. She asked Allah to bless me and keep me safe. She told me to close my eyes and count to one hundred. I did. The blindfold came off. I looked around and she was gone. And I was standing in the middle of the Hagia Sophia. I looked around and saw you," indicating Ed, "and came over. That's all I know."

Both Ed and I were silent.

"What happened to me? Why me? What's going on?" asked Andrew.

"Good questions," answered Ed.

"Perfectly good question," I added. "Now if we had a perfectly good answer!"

Ed arranged for Andrew to be checked by our medical crew and then taken back to his hotel by security where he would be watched for twenty four hours.

"Well, Pip, I've done what I can do tonight," he said.

"Right, let's get some sleep and come back to this in the morning," I replied. "Let's hope this was a fluke and no one else gets kidnapped . . ."

". . . And then rescued by some mysterious maiden," added Ed.

". . . Tomorrow or anytime during this conference."

I should have known better.

❁ Chapter Ten ❁

I went back to my apartment. As is my usual practice before I went to bed, I arranged and set out all of the notes and schedules I would need for the next day.

It was very late (some would argue 'early') when I tumbled into bed.

I dreamed of 'Sarah.' In my dream, I remember finding myself in a long winding tunnel. As I walked I heard singing so I followed the sound. I came to a large room lit by candles and filled with women of all ages and in varying styles of dress. They were smiling at me, beckoning me to come into the room. They were singing. I didn't catch the whole song; it seemed to be sung in many languages. I did understand one phrase, however. Indeed, I woke up singing it.

"We are all sisters,
One are we.
All sisters longing to be free.
Sarah our mother,
We raise her name,
Sarah, our sister . . ."

The rest eluded me. Now where in the world did that come from?

I showered and dressed and had a roll and apricot juice. Grabbing my briefcase I called downstairs for a cab and was on my way to the Hagia Sophia.

Chapter Eleven

The morning session was a great success. Of course, I might be a little biased but I thought it was wonderful. We began by listening to the choir from my home church in Minnesota singing an anthem titled, How Different Can We Be. Then we listened to six different folk telling of their experiences of faith. We broke into discussion groups so that all would have the opportunity to share their stories of faith. Many commented on how surprising it was that the stories were so similar. We concluded the session with a concert given by two musical groups. The first group presented three original musical numbers singing praise to Allah and calling for fellowship across religious lines. The last group, Peter, Paul and Mary, sang mixed Christian and Jewish folk songs. They concluded with the song, We Are One. It brought the house down! People stood with their arms around each other, hugging, laughing, even dancing. After three encores, we adjourned until tomorrow's sessions. These sessions would be spent planning strategies on how we might promote unity, peace and justice between our three religions.

As we dismissed to go to lunch, I could hear people discussing plans to meet together and sight see. They were making plans to spend the afternoon with their new friends.

Jack and Carolyn walked past me.

"Oh, Pip," said Carolyn. "That was just terrific. It was a good idea to have the music. It really brought people together.

Jack nodded his agreement. "We're going to lunch with a group of Muslims from Ghana. It will be the first time for most of them to have conversation with American Christians. Actually, probably any

Christians. It should be exciting. We'll see you this evening at the planning session."

They hurried along to meet their luncheon group.

I stood and watched the crowd of people leave. Earlier where I had seen many individuals, now I saw groups of people in conversation with each other. We had made a start!

As I stood aside to let people scurry by, I felt a darkness, a presence behind me. And then all was dark.

Chapter Twelve

I awoke with a pounding headache. I was bound hand and foot with a strip of duct tape over my mouth. "Not very original," I thought. As my eyes adjusted to the dimness of the room, or cave, or whatever it was, I took note of my surroundings. I was seated on some sort of wooden chair with arms to which my arms were bound. The room had one lamp or lantern which was set on a rickety table. I could see two steps leading up to a heavy wooden door. "So", I thought, "not the same place where Andrew had been kept."

As my head cleared, I realized that I was hearing footsteps coming toward me. The door opened and a beam of light shined into the room. I had a split second to decide – would I be awake or asleep. I chose to be asleep. I dropped my head, closed my eyes and slumped my body.

"She's still out. Man, how much of that stuff did you hit her with?" one raspy voice asked.

"I had to be sure she came quietly, didn't I?" answered the second higher pitched voice. "Anyway, why do we need her awake? The boss won't be here until tomorrow, so what's the hurry?"

"OK, I guess you're right. Just so she isn't dead," responded raspy voice. I could feel him lean over and check my pulse. "Nah, she's alive. So what do we do in the meantime?"

"What else?" answered high-pitched voice. "We wait. At least we can wait outside of this crummy place."

"The boss said to keep a close watch on her," said 'raspy.'

"OK, OK, we'll take turns and check on her every fifteen minutes. This place gives me the willies!"

"Sounds good to me. I mean even if she wakes up, where can she go?" the voice laughed.

"And ain't nobody gonna hear her, that's for sure."

They both laughed and stood there for a moment. Then I could hear their footsteps go back up the steps toward the door.

"This door is huge," said raspy voice.

"Yeah and heavy." I heard grunts as they must have opened the door.

"This room was a torture cell, I guess," answered 'high pitched;' the idea was to keep people in."

"I'm sure glad I don't have to be locked up in here," said 'raspy.' "It's bad enough to have to be checking on her . . ." as the door closed and I was left by myself. I waited a moment to be sure they were gone then opened my eyes and tried to focus and orient myself. My head was still buzzing and my arms and legs ached from being tied. I was stiff all over from being in the same painful position. "If I have to be here until the 'boss' comes tomorrow, I'm going to be in pretty bad shape," I thought. "Now think, Pip. Don't panic. What would James Bond do?"

Just as I was exerting what brain power I had to the problem, I heard a low scrapping behind me. Again I heard the sound and then felt a breath of fresh air. The lantern flickered and then held steady. I felt rather than heard someone come toward me.

In the brief two or three seconds between the scrapping sound and the revelation of the presence of someone I was busy praying.

"Oh, Lord, make me brave. Oh God, help me to act with courage. Oh God, help . . ."

A shadow leaned over me. With much trepidation, I opened my eyes and saw the loveliest young woman I have seen for a long time.

"Shhh," she said. "Make not a sound. I am here to help you," and with that, she cut the duct tape and rope that bound me. "We must go quickly," she gestured behind us to where I heard the scrapping sound.

"You must be Sarah," I guessed. "Somehow I'm not surprised to see you."

"You have been talking to Andrew," she responded. "Hush, now, we must get you away from here."

Hot needles stung my feet, legs and arms. My hands were burning. I hurt in places I didn't know I had.

The shadow stranger helped me to the back of the room where we exited between a narrow slit in the wall. After we were on the other side I heard the slow scrapping sound and watched the wall seal up behind us.

"We must move along quickly and quietly so we can't be sensed or heard," whispered my rescuer.

The tunnel-like hallway we were in merged with several other passageways and were lit with flickering torches hung on sconces along the walls.

As we walked along I noticed writings and carvings on the walls. We came to one that clearly was a name, a date and the sign of the cross. "Catacombs!" I exclaimed. "So this is what they were used for. Not torture chambers but sanctuaries!"

Sarah touched her finger to her lips signaling silence. As she did so she also nodded her head responding to my comment about the early Christian worship held here.

After we walked awhile we came to a small room. "This is where they held your young friend, Andrew," she indicated. "We must move along even more quickly now for they know of some of these passageways."

I moved as quickly as possible, the red-hot needles having now subsided to a prickly numbness. I leaned heavily on my guide. We came to a long flat wall surface. Somehow as we stood there the wall slid open and we crossed into a brightly lit passage. The wall slid closed behind us. We proceeded from the hallway into a large, well-lit, brightly decorated and comfortably furnished room.

"A restroom?" I asked urgently.

"Let me help you," responded an older woman coming to my aid.

The emergency dealt with, I returned to the large room and was shown to a comfortable chair around a wide, round table.

An elderly woman was seated at the table across from me. Others gathered around as well, until all ten of the seats were filled. The woman who had been seated first began.

"By now you are immensely curious. We will seek to satisfy your curiosity as best we can. First of all, let me assure you that you are safe and among friends. You are in the presence of members of an ancient organization called Sisters of Sarah. We are a sorority of women, Jewish, Muslim and Christian, who, over the ages, have sought to work for the education, well-being and, if necessary, the transportation of women to new locations. As you are celebrating in the conference above us, the relationship of Christian, Jew and Muslim through connectedness with Father Abraham, we celebrate the sisterhood of women under the banner of sister/mother Sarah. My name is Sarah and I am the mother of this House of Sarah. You are welcome here."

I looked around me at the faces of the women at the table. They came from many ethnic and cultural backgrounds as witnessed by their dress and beautiful and diverse faces. Some appeared to be in their twenties and the ages extended into later senior years.

I was overwhelmed by the whole situation.

As I tried to focus my mind and speech, the woman who had rescued me spoke.

"My name, too, is Sarah, as you know. I am the youngest member of this Sisters of Sarah House. That is why I was given the privilege of bringing you here. I am a Christian and I came from the United States. My father abused me and beat my mother to death. He sexually assaulted me and my baby sister as well. The welfare department took her away and she was placed in a foster home. They were going to come and get me the next day. My father heard about this and came out of hiding. When he found only me left at home, he became so enraged, he took me out to the shed and beat me with a baseball bat – the same way he killed my mother. As this was happening four women – I later learned that one of the welfare workers from the previous day was a messenger for the Sisters of Sarah – came, tied him up and left him for the authorities. Then they took me to a SOS safe house. That was six years ago. I have travelled an interesting journey with the Sisters and that journey has led me here to the Mother House. Here I am learning to read Hebrew, Arabic and French. I will become a teacher, I believe, and work out of a Sisters of Sarah House in one of the many cities where we work.

Currently our goal is to assist you and this conference, <u>ONE GOD: Many Names</u> to be successful and heard around the world."

Another woman, speaking with an African dialect accent continued.

"We have watched with interest the planning of this conference. Some of your planning committee are members of the sisterhood."

I could tell there was a great look of surprise on my face. "You mean. . . ."

"Not now, dear," responded Mother Sarah. "All in good time, perhaps, when there is time."

"But how have you survived all these years and how have you kept the secret?" I asked.

"Allah is good," responded one of the women. "And we have many wise friends. . ."

"And with friends come connections," added Mother Sarah. She smiled at me and said, "Another time, dear."

As we sat around the table I was introduced to these Sisters of Sarah. Each told the story of how she had come to the sisterhood. They were from South Africa, Saudi Arabia, Turkey, the U.S.A., Israel, Egypt, Iran, Somalia and Italy. They were students, doctors, investment counselors, teachers, cooks and housekeepers. All had been educated by the Sisters of Sarah. Currently they were all headquartered here but were subject to be transferred where their skills were most needed.

"We are gathered here at this time to lend aid and support to your seminar. We have been vigilant in watching events unfold. That is why we were able to come to your aid so rapidly. As we sit here the two who snatched you. . ."

"Ol' raspy voice and high-pitched voice. . ." I muttered to myself.

". . . Are being secreted out of the Sophia and into the arms of the Metropolitan Police and the custody of Inspector Majed Musa.

"Majed!" I exclaimed. "Does he know about this?"

"But of course," replied Mother Sarah. "He is the reason we were able to find you so quickly. Do you remember, perhaps, a small item he gave you in the garden?"

"Of course. The little cell-phone-kind of thing. That's how you found me?"

"Yes, it was very fortunate you had it on you . . ."

". . . In my purse . . ." which I held up for them to see. The little transceiver-phone, whatever, was still in the small side pocket where I'd placed it and promptly forgotten about it.

"Answer me this. Does Majed know about the Sisters of Sarah?"

"He does," answered one of the women at the table. "I am from Istanbul. My name is Iszmae. Majed is my husband. We have two daughters. One is named Lola and one named Sarah. Yes, Majed knows all about the Sisters of Sarah!" She laughed and patted me on the arm. "And now you know about us as well."

"But where do we go from here?" I asked. "Who is behind all of this? What more have they planned? What should I do now?"

Mother Sarah rose from her chair and crossed to me. She put her hand on my arm, looked into my eyes and said, "You will remain with us for the day where we can support you and care for your wounds. Then you will return to the conference tomorrow well, energized and fresh. No more questions for now. Place everything in my hands. You may trust me completely, dear."

I did trust her! It was amazing because just thirty minutes ago I'd never met her nor heard of the Sisters of Sarah.

The rest of my day was spent in luxury! I was provided a lovely scented bath followed by a warm oils massage. I was re-hydrated with fresh fruit juice and cool lemon water. After awhile one of the sisters brought me clean clothes from my apartment. How did they know, I wondered.

"I need to contact some folks. You know, make arrangements, to be sure everything is going as planned, touch base," I said to one of the sisters caring for me.

"I am Esther," she responded. "You need not worry about anything. All has been cared for."

"But people will wonder where I am. They'll need to hear from me," I protested.

"All is cared for," repeated Esther gently. "Everyone on your team has gotten an email from you with suggestions, comments and a note saying you were doing some sight seeing and visiting old friends. Everything is on schedule. Now you may rest for an hour or so and then we will meet with the Sisterhood's council and evaluate next steps." And with that, the lights were dimmed, soft music drifted across the room...

Humph, a couple of emails and I'm replaced! So much for thinking I was indispensible!

The music and the dim lights were effective. I floated into a peaceful, restful afternoon nap.

Chapter Thirteen

I awoke remarkably refreshed. I had expected to be stiff and sore but as I stood up I felt relaxed and pain free, better even than I had felt prior to being drugged and bound. I walked across the room, glancing at the paintings on the wall. I came to a bookshelf with an interesting looking manuscript of some five hundred pages. As I thumbed through it, I realized it was the story of the Sisters of Sarah. Obviously it had been left for me to read. I sat in a comfortable chair and began. It only took a page or two to draw me into the story. Mother Sarah said I would be given answers and here they were. The organization was begun in the early seventh century here in Istanbul. I was amazed at their singular sense of purpose of uplifting women, educating, freeing and giving them new opportunities. Throughout years, centuries, long before anyone else, the Sisters of Sarah have been faithful to their chosen task of women's lib! Apparently they have used an ever-expanding base of knowledge and technology that is now made available to them.

I was so immersed in my reading that I lost all track of time until one of the sisters brought me a tray with a light meal. She was about to leave when I asked if she would stay and talk with me.

"Surely I will," she answered in a very cultured British-sounding voice. "I am Marta," she continued. "Come, my sister, eat the meal that has been prepared for you. We can converse as you eat." She sat down beside me and lifted the cover on the tray. A veritable bouquet of wonderful smelling foods filled the room. There was roasted chicken, fresh bread, butter, honey, olives, cheese, yogurt, vegetable salad and a beautiful, warm pastry with an apricot center. Of course, there was freshly brewed Chia and a carafe of iced water with lemon.

"I can't eat all this," I said. "You must share with me."

We sat together eating and trading stories of our families. Marta came from a poor family in London. She was the youngest of eleven. When she was nine, her father arranged for her to get into 'the trade.'

"I was fortunate," continued Marta. "The madam in our house was kind to me and saw to it that I was educated and could speak well. After three years I discovered a neighborhood house that welcomed me. It was an SOS home. I eventually went to live there after my madam died and her 'house' was broken up. Several pimps were looking for me, but the sisters kept me safe. For my own safety, I was sent first to an SOS in Holland and then when my skill in languages was realized, I was sent to the mother house here in Istanbul. I speak seven languages – Turkish, English, French, German, Dutch, Arabic and Spanish. I've been working on one of the teams on your planning committee. I volunteered to serve. I think your committee has found me very useful."

"I can imagine!" I responded. "How long have you been serving on one of our committees?"

"I'm on the Hospitality Committee," she said. "I was the first recruit that Karl and Hannah got to serve on their team."

"You mean Karl and Hannah know about the Sisters of Sarah?" I asked.

"Oh, no, they just know that I'm an interpreter and could be helpful to them." She smiled. "A mutual friend introduced us."

"And this mutual friend is a sister?" I questioned.

"Now Dr. Pip, you should finish your meal. We have much to do this evening."

I took the hint.

Chapter Fourteen

The committee meeting had been set for 8:00 p.m. at the reception hall in the Hagia Sophia. I arrived a few minutes early and was seated at the table when the others arrived.

I heard "hello." Looking around me I was surprised to find Marta seated next to me. She smiled and winked at me.

Jack and Carolyn were bubbling with enthusiasm about their meal and time together with ten representatives from Ghana. They sat down and told me about their meal.

"We were very polite and, well, distant at first," said Carolyn. "But as the meal progressed . . ."

"And no one clobbered each other . . ." added Jack.

". . . We got friendlier and more open. It was a wonderful time of coming together and sharing."

"God only knows what stories they had been told of what to expect from the greedy, cold and not-to-be trusted American Christians." And after some thought, "I am amazed that they were even willing to go out to eat with us."

"Surprising that they even would come to this conference," added Carolyn.

"I think they're hungry for peace and fellowship as well as we. Anyway, I think we dispelled some of the suspicion," Jack said with satisfaction.

We talked some more as the other committee members arrived and were seated.

Our group this evening consisted of the following team leaders and members:

Ed Arnold – security
Jack and Carolyn Anderson – registration and program
Marta Christian – hospitality and interpreter
Muhammad Musa – registrar
Hakim Rakin – financial manager
Karl and Hannah Ridlington – hospitality
Rosa Steinfelt – hotel hospitality
Jacob Schmidt – program
Shakira Abdul – program
Nathan Greenblat – program/resources
Almir Majad – program/resources
Carin Nelson-Anderson – program/resources
And myself, general chair

Each person made a brief report and then I asked for general comments and impressions of the conference so far.

"I thought the music added a real nice touch," responded Rosa. "I liked it and thought most people could relate to it. It was a real communication builder."

"The meals and the tours have been an extra plus," said Hakim. "I know that these have helped there to be an atmosphere of, how should I say it, friendship and mutuality."

There was general agreement around the room. Most added comments and constructive criticism and many had ideas for 'next time.'

"Do you think there will be a next time?" I asked.

"Count on it, Dr. Pip," answered Shakira. "Now that we have made such a successful start we must surely continue."

"I believe our voices will be heard," added Jacob. "We are a part of something bigger and more important than any of us as individuals."

All around the table I saw nodding heads and words of affirmation.

"All the programs and plans are prepared and ready for the next two days?" I asked.

We proceeded to put what finishing touches were needed on the last days of the conference. Following that we adjourned. Several members were planning a late-night meal together.

"Dr. Pip, won't you come with us?" asked Almir.

I was about to respond by saying I was tired and thought I'd go to bed when the door opened and Majed came in. He beckoned to Ed and me.

"May I have a word?" he asked.

I said good bye to the others as they went off to have a relaxing meal with each other. I knew they were tired, too, and this time together would do them good.

"See you tomorrow," I said as they left. After they were gone, Ed, Majed and I sat down at the table.

"What can I do for you?" I asked.

"We've been talking with the two thugs who tied you up," answered Majed.

"Wait does Ed know . . .?" I asked.

"Yes, Pip, Majed has kept me apprised of everything," responded Ed. He continued, "Just exactly what did they tell you?"

"They didn't say much at all except that the 'boss' wouldn't get here until tomorrow," I answered. I told them everything I remembered of their conversation, but there wasn't really much to tell. It seemed obvious that they were not the instigators of the plot but rather paid flunkies.

"I'm running a profile on them now," added Majed. "I suspect we'll find the usual type wrap sheet on them. Pretty typical brawn but not much brain for hire."

"The question is who will arrive at the conference tomorrow?" I asked.

"I can answer that," responded Ed. "I've got a list of nine late-shows, all of whom have just arrived or will arrive in time for tomorrow." He held up a file with a list of names and information of the latest additions to the conference.

"Of course, it's always possible that the 'boss' isn't a registered attendee of the conference. It could be someone who just happens to be in Istanbul coincidentally, like," added Majed.

"That is a possibility that we can't overlook," answered Ed. "My money is on one of these, however," indicating the list in his hand. "Why don't you look over these names, Pip? Do you recognize any of them?"

He handed me the list.

"Numbers one and two are somewhat familiar to me. Number one, Dr. Ezra Graham, is a professor of Middle East Culture and Religion at Cambria University in Virginia. Number two, Dr. Aria Herman, is associate professor of Hebrew Studies at Jewish University in Joppa. She is an outspoken critic of current Israeli policies. Numbers three through seven are unknown to me. To my knowledge, I've never met or heard of them. The last two names are a bit of a surprise to me, however."

"Here," I said, "number eight is the Rev. Hollis Freeborn. He's a self-proclaimed 'expert' on 'false religious teachings.' As far as I know he has no academic credentials. His main theme is that Christians are superior to Jews and Muslims. They all, Jews and Muslims, and, incidentally 'liberal' Christians, fall into his category of 'unsavable.' Even if they should convert or repent, they are still looked upon as 'fallen' and 'lost,' his words, not mine. He has a small but faithful group of followers. They call themselves the 'Children of the Light' because, presumably, they battle the darkness of false religious teaching. I've heard him speak and he seems to me to be pretty much a 'loose cannon.' I wouldn't actually think him capable of an organized plot but then I really don't know him."

"And number nine?" posed Ed.

"Yes, my old 'friend,' Dr. Ibraham El-Hamin. I certainly can't prove anything, but, frankly, if there is a plot to discredit or destroy this conference or anything having to do with cooperation, communication and understanding between Muslims and anyone I wouldn't be surprised if Ibraham had a hand in it. He is not Al-Quada. He's pretty much independent of them, doesn't trust anyone, I think. He does hate Americans, Christians, Jews, liberal Muslims – you name it, he doesn't trust it. Mostly, I believe, he is fueled by his hatred for Americans. Oh yes, he doesn't care very much for me, either."

"In other words, he bears watching," said Majed.

"Yes, definitely, if you can. But I would imagine he has already 'disappeared' from plain sight. He likes to travel in the shadows, so to speak," I replied.

"Well, now, what should we do with Musa and Fred?" asked Ed.

"Who?" I asked.

"You know, the two guys who drugged you and . . ."

"Oh yeah."

"We will hold them in one of our 'special' cells," responded Majed. "Often times people can be convinced to say many things rather than have to stay in that place."

"Now Majed, I'm opposed to torture," I urged.

"As am I, Pip. This is not torture. It is just gloomy and sort of scary, as you Americans might say." He laughed, ever so slightly.

"I don't know," I hesitated.

"Do it," said Ed. "The more information we have, the better."

We got up to leave.

"Pip, you need to watch your step. Have you got that little receiver Majed gave you?" asked Ed.

"I do," I answered. "And believe me, I will stay in a group of folks at the conference."

Ed left with the list of new arrivals. "I've got my work cut out for me."

Majed lingered for a moment.

"And I, too, have much to do," he said. And, as if it were an afterthought, he leaned over to me and whispered, "Don't be too frightened, Pip. I have it on good authority that you are now in the care and protection of the Sisters of Sarah. Whoever it is who wish you harm might themselves be in for a big surprise."

With that he winked at me and was out the door.

Amazingly, I felt safe!

Chapter Fifteen

The next day was filled with fun and exciting classes and displays.

The three classes were held three different times to allow for attendance at all of them if you liked. They were 'basic' beginner classes titled Christianity 101, Islam 101 and Judaism 101. I could see they were well attended and heard from those attending that they were interesting and informative, with lively discussions.

Everyone was also encouraged to visit the craft displays and food booths.

"Pip," I heard my name called by so many. "What a wonderful and fun idea to be able to go at our own speed and interest," said Andy Jacobs from England.

I particularly thought the hospitality committee had done a great job by setting up booths around the 'Sophia" with ethnic foods. There were typical Turkish breakfasts and samples of Jewish holiday dishes. One booth even had traditional Christmas goodies which our Jewish and Muslim friends certainly enjoyed! I personally sampled Norwegian yulekaaka, rosettes, krumkaaka and several other Christmas cookies. No lutefisk was served, however.

As I was strolling along, investigating each booth, I heard a voice calling me from across the way.

"Dr. Franzen, oh, Dr. Franzen, a word with you, please." Soon the voice came closer and with it appeared a rather short, plump, somewhat disheveled man.

"Why, Rev. Freeborn, I didn't really expect to see you here, of all places," I said. I've learned long ago that the handshake had originated in the middle ages when, upon meeting your enemies, you and they extended your arm to prove that you were unarmed, or at least swordless. It seemed the thing to do with Rev. Freeborn.

He acknowledged my held-out hand with a grunt and a look of suspicion and disdain. I wanted to assure him that I'd had all my shots but, well, the moment passed so quickly as he hurriedly went into his prepared speech.

"I am not in favor of this kind of gathering. Indeed I believe that God is not pleased with this meeting. God does not intend his true children to mingle with these . . . these others," he shuddered as he gazed around the area at Christians actually engaging with Jews and Muslims. "It's abhorrent, it's against nature and the will of God," he concluded.

"And the reason you're here today, Mr. Freeborn?" I asked. "Since you find it so abhorrent to 'mingle,' I believe that was your word. Why are you here at all?"

"I'm here to preach the word! To say to all who will listen that this is a dangerous, God-less gathering of people who are sinners, yes, sinners, all of you!"

He looked around and must have noticed a crowd gathering around us. As if on cue, he 'took stage,' leaping up the two steps of the entryway, speaking loudly and gesturing wildly.

"Repent before it's too late. God looks upon this gathering as an abomination, only true Christians can be saved, don't stain your souls with the godless . . ." He was about to continue his tirade when several of the conference attendees 'booed' him down. Others joined them and soon he was surrounded by a crowd of folk loudly disagreeing with him. In a matter of minutes the security force came and took Mr. Freeborn from where he was 'preaching.'

After he left and the crowd had quieted down, one of those attending the conference, a middle-aged Arabic woman, stood where Freeborn had been standing. She began speaking to those around her.

"Dear friends both old and new. Up until now I have pretty much been silent. I was afraid to speak my feelings. But now I need to speak out loud my thoughts."

The crowd began to listen in earnest. The room grew quiet.

"I am Esther. I live here in Istanbul. My daughter brought me here today. I have faith that many of you, like me, are here today because you share many of the same feelings my daughter and I share. We are faithful followers of Islam. The babble that man was shouting, that is what we stand against. It is that kind of confused thinking, no, it is more than that. It is evil set upon us to confuse and divide us. But today, now, forever, I declare to all of you that although we call God by different names, we worship but one God. I believe this with all my heart and I will work the rest of my life to spread this word."

Esther stood down and was immediately enfolded in the arms of her daughter. They both were weeping tears of joy. The crowd broke into applause, cheers, and shouts of affirmation, hugging and handshakes.

Poor Mr. Freeborn – he had accomplished exactly the opposite of what he had intended.

One could pity him, almost.

❁ Chapter Sixteen ❁

It was about an hour after the "Freeborn Incident," as I now thought of it. Ed Farnum caught my attention as the crowds of people moved from coffee break to sessions on the three faiths. There were also several sessions of people beginning to strategize next steps as we seek to find more and more ways to peacefully spread our message.

"Pip," he said, and motioned me over toward his security office. "You'll be interested in knowing the information we've elicited from Hollis Freeborn."

I sat down next to Ed's desk.

"OK, fill me in," I said.

"First of all, the man is not a reverend anything. He has a high school diploma from a small school in West Virginia. Then he had a month or two of trade school in carpentry. After that he was in the Army for two years when he served as a chaplain's assistant. That's apparently where he picked up some of the jargon. To make a long story short, Mr. Freeborn came here not to preach the word. That was just a cover-up for the real reason which was to 'rescue' his son from being kidnapped."

"Ahh," I thought, beginning to see the light. "His son wouldn't be named Andrew Whitaker by any chance, would he?"

"Correct. Andrew chose to keep his mother's maiden name after she had an apparently bitter divorce from Freeborn. Andrew enrolled at Yale where he's doing work on ecumenism. Freeborn became concerned, more like enraged, that his son has 'fallen off the pathway of God.' He decided to have him kidnapped. Then he could rush in and save Andrew all the while placing the blame on the perverts and sinners who are sponsoring this conference. We haven't gotten all the details but that's pretty much how it plays out."

"Have you re-united the two yet?"

"I was just going to. Do you want to be there?"

"No. At least for Andrew's sake if not for Freeborn's sake, we need to give them some privacy." Ed nodded in agreement.

"But Ed, maybe someone should talk to Andrew first. This whole thing can't be a very happy situation for him."

"I'm already ahead of you, Pip. Andrew is talking with one of the counselors here for the conference. Actually, it's one of his professors at school."

"It's sad, isn't it?" I commented. "A father kidnapping his own son to do what? Prove he's right and the son wrong? With just the opposite effect, I think."

"That's probably only part of it," suggested Ed.

"Hopefully Andrew will follow up with some more counseling at school."

"That does solve one mystery, though, doesn't it?"

"Yes, one."

Chapter Seventeen

ISTANBUL, 1736 C.E.

(Excerpt from personal journal, Sisters of Sarah, Mother Sarah, Istanbul, December 22, 1736.)

I have just returned from my travels to many of our SOS houses across the continent. There is so much turmoil in our world. Unfortunately, that being the case, women often bear much of the burden from that turmoil.

As members of the Sisterhood, we seek to alleviate the pain and sorrow that seems to fall upon women. I have seen much suffering in the past few months as I traveled throughout the countryside. I was able to rescue ten young women. They are now placed in several of our homes for education, safety, nourishment and a future. They were given their choice as to where they would be placed. Three of these young women were orphans aged nine, eleven and fourteen. They will do well together in the SOS house in Vienna. I believe they might do well as nurses; time will tell.

I found two young women in a brothel in Paris. I was able to pay for their release from their madam. They have been placed in our home in Rome. If they have the aptitude, they will be educated in the arts.

The other five were taken from the streets of London. They survived as they could. Now they will be kept safe and educated as seamstresses, cooks and nannies. Placed in the homes of the members of the Sisterhood, of course.

It is good to see the fresh possibilities of these young women. And sad, no, tragic, to know that there are so many we are unable to reach. But we will keep trying!

I have personally begun the task of preparing the next Mother Sarah. I believe she may well be ready to assume her duties in a year. She does well in her studies and excels in Arabic and English. We will look forward to her leadership. I remember well when we took her from the streets of Paris. She was five years old and all alone, standing next to the body of her mother. We can only guess at her story before she came to us. And now she has grown and matured, ready to take new responsibilities upon her shoulders. And to be perfectly straightforward, I am looking forward to assuming less demanding responsibilities with the Sisters of Sarah.

Sister Sarah XXXX

NOTE: Remember to go over report of Sister Leala Rose with her. Rumors about the city speculate that there are secret passages under the 'Sophia" (which, of course, is true). We must decide to allow them to 'discover' the two most vulnerable rooms – the old torture room and the other cell along the same wall. Let them 'find' them and perhaps they will be satisfied.

NOTE: Fortunately, the only rooms 'discovered' were those we allowed to be found. The Sisters of Sarah headquarters remain a secret to this day.

Sister Sarah IIVL

❁ Chapter Eighteen ❁

"Majed, Ed, if the two kidnappings were perpetrated by two different groups for two different reasons," I postulated.

"Yes, yes, Dr. Pip," reflected Majed. "The first by Freeborn to try to gain favor with his estranged son and the second to . . ."

". . . To reflect badly, maybe even ruin the conference, being planned by . . ."

". . . Whomever. OK, so two different kidnappings. How do they know about the secret rooms under the Sophia?" I asked. "And if they know about the rooms, as they seem to, do they know about the Sisters? Or, for some weird reason, are the Sisters behind all of this for their own reasons? I hate to even suggest that but, well . . ."

"Yes, of course," responded Majed. "We must examine the puzzle from all sides."

"But you don't think the Sisters of Sarah are in any way involved in my kidnapping, do you?" I asked.

"No, I don't," he answered. "But you must be completely satisfied that they are who they say they are and not out to harm you or this conference."

"I remember reading in one of the journals of Sisters. It said, to the effect that the 'outside world,' or at least some elements of the outside world. . . ."

". . . The underworld," added Ed.

"Yes, well, that there were certain people who knew about and used these secret chambers for their own nefarious deeds. Is that still true, Majed?"

"I know of their existence and certain other members of the police force suspect and have heard rumors of them. And, of course, other people know of them."

"If that is so, why aren't they closed?" I asked.

"There has been no real investigation regarding their existence. Just rumors, stories, you know, ghost stories related to the Aya Sophia, mostly," he answered.

"Could the Sisters block them off?" asked Ed.

"They could but then they wouldn't be able to rescue those who were being tortured or locked in there," responded Majed.

"Case in point . . ." and he gestured toward me.

"I gottcha," I nodded.

Chapter Nineteen

Just as I was preparing to go back to my apartment I heard, "Pip, I've been looking for you." Recognizing the voice, I turned around and saw Ali coming toward me on the run. Just as he got close to me, three large gentlemen grabbed him and forced him to the floor as they pushed me aside.

"We have him," declared one of the men. "Cuff him and we'll..."

"Wait just a minute," I said, finally realizing that the three were members of the security force.

"You've just wrestled to the ground the Turkish Minister of Finance. Hopefully he will not bring charges and that this will not cause an international incident!" I began to laugh. Ali, too, was laughing as they released him. One of the men tried to brush off his suit as he apologized.

"I'm so sorry, sir. We were instructed to keep Dr. Franzen safe."

"That's alright," responded Ali. "I'm glad to see that you take your job seriously. I feel like I've been tackled by Reggie White of the Green Bay Packers." He shook hands with his tacklers and then came over to me.

"Word has it that a substantial amount of money has been removed from one account to another as payment to see that you and your conference are not successful," he said.

I looked at him speculatively and he responded, "Don't ask me how I know. Actually, I shouldn't know. Just believe me. So, what's going on with you?" quickly changing the subject.

Since I've known and trusted Ali for many years, I gave him a quick once-over about what had transpired in the past days, leaving out only the part about the Sisters of Sarah.

"I thought it might be something like that," he said. "I, too, have heard the stories of the secret rooms beneath the Sophia. The rumors ebb and flow, depending on what's happening on the political scene. Well, here I am. What can I do to help?"

By this time, the crowd that had gathered began to disperse and we were left, Ali, myself and the three security guards. As we were talking, Majed and Ed sprinted across the room to meet us.

I was saying, "Tonight we have our big gathering. Sort of a grand finale. Everyone will be together here at the Sophia. There will be speeches, singing and a lot of fellowship. It will be the last official event of the conference."

"And the last opportunity for someone to disrupt and cause chaos," warned Ed, meaningfully.

As we were talking, several of the planning committee came over. Muhammad Musa, our registrar, came up to me and said, "I believe I have all the final numbers. We have six hundred and forty two people registered as conference attendees. There are also forty members of the various media, twenty five observers and thirty or so visiting family members. I think that we've done very well for our first time. As you can see," handing me a sheet of paper, "I have compiled the country of origin and religious preference as well. It is quite an interesting mix."

"Thank you, Muhammad, for your fine work. We'll be able to use these figures as we plan for other conferences and events. We couldn't have done it without you," I commented.

"Do we have time for something to eat?" asked Ali.

Ed looked at his watch and answered, "Yes, good idea!"

"I'm hungry! Let's go, shall we," I replied. "I haven't been out of here all day. I don't even know what the weather has been doing all day."

As it ended up, there were ten of us going together. We had a great time relaxing, eating some fine Turkish meals and going over the events of the last few days. We finished in plenty of time to return to the Sophia for the closing ceremony at 8:00 p.m.

Chapter Twenty

As we arrived back at the Sophia, people had begun to gather. Smiles were on faces as people greeted new friends and old. This evening's program was loosely organized to give folks a chance to review and remember, to plan and to celebrate. We were going to have some music. Some speakers talked of their planned 'next steps,' a five-minute video with members of the Jewish, Muslim and Christian faiths and some last minute data reporting by Muhammad about numbers and projecting our next meeting. Then I would say a few words of greeting and invite those in attendance to our next WE Conference to be held in two years in London.

It was exciting and gratifying to listen to the 'next steps' planned by many of the conference attendees.

"I plan to hold a series of tea and discussion groups with my Christian neighbors," said one Muslim housewife from Brighton, England.

"I've got a craft shop. I'm going to exhibit arts and crafts from our many ethnic groups. And, oh yes, talk with people," responded a Jewish merchant from Rome.

Classes, phone calls, lunches, letters, tea parties, letters to the editor – the suggestions ranged from very simple to elaborate (a ten-day tour of Christian, Jewish and Muslim holy sights). Students would research and march. Professors would listen and teach and collaborate. People would speak up. People would support one another. They would visit places of worship and invite each other to their services of study and worship. We would use common terms such as prayer, peace, love, compassion, God and so many others. And we would hold these new friends and all we'd learned and shared in our thoughts and prayers.

As our conference was drawing to a close, I could feel the energy arising from the crowd. I also began to breathe easier.

"We're almost there," I thought to myself. "Almost with no major incident, almost there. . ."

I rose to speak one last time. As I stood, three masked men (women? but they seemed to be men) ran out in front of me with automatic weapons in their hands. They shouted in English for us to be quiet. Then they came and stood around me, pointing their guns in my face.

As I stood there, the crowd parted and I saw coming toward the dais, a tall man, covered with a full black face mask. He was followed by four other masked men with guns. They stood in front of where I was standing and raised their weapons toward the crowd.

"Now, in front of these people and before Allah, denounce this conference and what it stands for or I will order my followers to shoot as many of your people as they can. We will slaughter them, do you hear? And it will be your fault. The guilt will fall upon you, you foolish woman, you daughter of evil, you unbeliever," came the voice, loudly projected in some way throughout the whole Aya Sophia. And again he spoke.

"We will kill you all and you, daughter of hell, will watch it happen. The world will hate you. It will despise you and never listen to your words of cunning again. You mislead my people. You smooth talk the world into believing your plan to unite these people. You are a false prophet. You are a coward hiding behind the mistaken faith of others. All these people will die because of you," he continued to rant on as I stood there.

"Oh God, show me what to do," not realizing I was speaking out loud.

"Hah! You call to your God. He cannot help you. There is no God but Allah. You pray in vain to a non-existent god," and he laughed menacingly.

I was trying to remain calm, to think logically, but of course, logic was not what I was dealing with. Hence, "Perhaps I can convince them, give them my life for these others. Yes, that's what I will do," I thought.

I stepped forward.

"You don't really want to harm all these people. I believe it is me you're after. Why don't you . . ."

The air was rift with a sound as of thunder and great rumbling. It felt as if the whole building shook. I was thrown to the floor. The last thing I remember was the thought, "Oh no, they've used bombs;" then, for me, silence and darkness.

I awoke in the room beneath the Sophia where I had spent such a pleasant afternoon.

"Lie still. You must not strain yourself, Dr. Pip. You are safe now. The conference was a success. You don't need to worry." Mother Sarah was leaning over me. She had a soft, perfumed cloth with which she was gently wiping my hands, arms and face.

"What happened?" I asked, struggling to focus through the fog that seemed to engulf me.

"Your security forces led by Ed Arnold and our good friend, Majed, have the gunmen in custody. All is safe and calm," she replied.

"But what . . ." I sputtered.

"You must rest now," she soothed. "When you are able, all will be made clear. But now you must close your eyes. We don't want you to have a headache," and with that my eyelids, seemingly on command, closed. I remember spinning into darkness thinking, "They've put me to sleep, I wonder what drug . . ." then nothing.

ISTANBUL, 2005 C.E.

All is well at last. We have rooted out a ruthless gang of assassins in their attempt to vilify and destroy the efforts of Dr. Pip and her committee as they seek to bring harmony, understanding and fellowship between our three religions. The "WE" experience will continue and spread, thanks be to God and a goodly number of faithful coworkers in the Sisterhood and on committees. Our plans were effective and all was accomplished in relative secrecy.

The Sisters of Sarah became aware of Ibraham el-Hamin fifteen years ago. He was instrumental in creating confusion and spreading hatred in several of the cities in which we have SOS houses. Since that time, we have carefully monitored his activities. Up until three years ago, he was a professor of Islamic History at a small Islamic school in Afghanistan. Then, three years ago, he disappeared. We later found him leading a small group of his students in attacks and raids on anything he considered 'American.'

Funding evidently came from thieving, drugs and small arms sales. About three weeks ago, one of our friends in Cairo noticed him in a hotel. We followed up on this lead and have been observing him ever since. Actually, more than observing. Two of his group of assassins are in actual fact close associates of the SOS in Cairo. That explains the fact that this raid and attempted slaughter of so many was a failure. Our friends were in charge of acquiring and hiding the weapons in the lower secret rooms of the Sophia. Strangely, when the time came, all of the guns either misfired or didn't fire at all. Ibraham el-Hamin is now in the custody of Majed's Special Forces and his organization has been effectively neutralized.

As to the rest, I cannot say. Did Jesus, Abraham and Mohammad actually appear together at the close of the "WE" experience? There are those who are convinced they did. And the stories of Dr. Pip being lifted up and carried away to be protected by the three? Well, they are, after all, just stories.

The Sisters of Sarah continue to learn, change and expand. But always, always, we seek to serve the cause of women around the world. Women who seek unity, knowledge, peace and justice.

Chapter Twenty-One

I awoke in my little apartment back at the University. The room was filled with members of the planning committees. Then I heard a familiar voice, "Mom, I'm so glad you're alright," followed by my daughter Sarah sitting on the bed hugging me.

"How did you get here so soon?" I asked.

"So soon," replied Sarah. "But, Mom, we've been here three days waiting for you to wake up."

"We?" I asked. As soon as I looked around I knew, I could tell he was there.

"Lanny," I said.

"Yes, I'm here. But then you knew I'd be here," he added. He knelt down beside the bed and gave me a big Lanny-Bear squeeze.

And then another voice, not so familiar.

"Alright folks. This is Dr. Pip's nurse maid and doctor. It's time to get back to business," instructed LeeAnn, with Ali at her side ushering folks out the door.

"Business? What business?" I asked.

"No details for you yet," responded Ali.

"But just to bring you briefly into the loop, we've begun planning for the next WE Experience..."

"And Mom, they've moved it up a year in your honor!" It's going to be in Cairo, we've been invited and . . ."

"That's enough about that for now," said Lanny with finality. By now all but Lanny, Sarah, Ali and LeeAnn had left the room.

"So where's Kiri," I asked.

"She couldn't get away. You know she'll be leaving for London next week for her work-study program. She'll see you in about two weeks when you have a two-day layover in London on your way home," explained Lanny.

"OK you guys. Explain – tell me what happened," I asked. "I remember up until when those thugs appeared and waved their guns around, threatening everyone in the place. Then a roar, smoke and everything seemed to shudder, and darkness. That's it. That's all I remember."

Ali begun, "You fell to the floor. In the middle of the smoke and darkness the security forces merged on the gunmen who, by the way, for some reason were unable to fire a shot . . ."

". . . Some people say that Allah intervened," interjected Sarah, smiling.

Ali smiled and winked at me. "After the security force . . ."

"Yeah, all forty of them," chuckled Lanny. "The assassins didn't stand a chance."

"Well, anyway, with the terrorists in hand . . ."

"Mom, it all happened so fast you wouldn't believe it. During all this, some people said they saw three images. Everyone thinks it was Abraham, Jesus and Mohammed. They heard them talking . . ."

". . . In Hebrew, Greek and Arabic, I suppose," I added.

"Yes, how did you know," commented LeeAnn, seriously.

"Lucky guess," I answered.

"Anyway, Mom, all three figures spoke to the crowd and encouraged them to work for peace. Then they swooped down and swish, you disappeared. It was spectacular!" concluded Sarah.

"And how do you know all this, Sarah?" I asked.

"Oh, umm, I heard a lot of people talking about what happened."

"You almost sound as if you were there," I suggested.

"What? Me there? Ahh, of course not. Don't be silly, how could I have been there? Umm, no I wasn't here, I just heard a lot of stuff and then I . . ."

Ali interrupted our conversation with, "Oh no, she wasn't here. But you should rest, Pip. Yes, that's a good idea. Why don't you rest now?"

LeeAnn quickly seconded the motion and added that we might all meet here later for a light evening meal.

"For now, Mom, you rest. Dad hasn't ever been in Istanbul before today. I'm going to take him around to see some of the sights."

"Don't worry, Pip," added Ali. "You won't be alone. Your apartment is being watched twenty-four hours. But I'm pretty convinced that the threat is over with the arrest of El-Hamin.

Lanny and Sarah said they'd be back in time for our meal together. They invited LeeAnn to go with them. She looked at Ali and then me.

"Please go," I said. "I'll be fine."

"Yes, you go ahead," added Ali. "I'll stay here with Pip for awhile."

Sarah, Lanny and LeeAnn said their goodbyes, promising to be back in plenty of time to prepare dinner.

"We'll be sure to have something caramel for dessert," promised LeeAnn, knowing Ali's love of caramel.

"And how about something chocolate," asked Lanny. Lanny loves the five food groups – fried chicken, pizza, spaghetti, raspberries and chocolate.

"Yes, yes, we'll get chocolate," mused Sarah. Actually, Sarah loves chocolate as well.

They left laughing and planning.

"We shouldn't miss the Cisterns . . ."

". . . And also Topkapi . . ."

After they were gone, Ali turned to me and said, "I wouldn't question Sarah too much about where we were and what she was doing the days before and after the conference.

"What are you talking about?" I asked. Then I say the look on Ali's face. "You mean . . ."

He nodded. "After all," he continued, "she was in Istanbul for some length of time when she was going to school at the University."

"Do you mean to tell me that you think Sarah, my Sarah, is a member of the Sisters of Sarah? But I would know, I'd surely know that she . . ."

"And do you know everything she does and thinks, Pip?" he asked.

"Wait a minute. Wait just a minute. How do you know about any of this? I purposely left out the Sisters of Sarah stuff when I talked to you"

"Yes, and I appreciate that. We knew you could be trusted by your careful telling and not telling parts of the story," he said.

I sat quietly for a moment, digesting our conversation and its implications.

"Ali, how do you know? How much do you know?"

"I pretty much know everything. How do you suppose I got to be Minister of Finance at so young an age?"

"The Sisters of Sarah . . .?"

". . . Are a very influential and powerful political force," he said. "All the more so because they are not public. They work behind the scenes. How else could I be in such an 'inside' position?"

"Yes, and very helpful to the Sisters, I am sure," I reflected.

"Oh, it's pretty much a mutual arrangement," he said, smiling.

"How did you know about them in the first place?" I asked.

"My mother and her mother and her mother," he answered. "And don't forget I have a sister named Sarah."

"Getting back to my Sarah," I insisted. "Where is she in all of this?"

"That you must ask her," he answered. "You might be interested to know that there are now new SOS houses in Uzbekistan and Cape Verde," he said with a twinkle in his eye. "Of course they are just new and beginning but word has it that they are doing promising work!"

Sarah had been posted in Uzbekistan and Cape Verde while serving in the Peace Corps two years ago.

Chapter Twenty-Two

The meal was delicious and the conversation lively. Ali had invited Majed and his wife Iszmae to join us. Ed Arnold was also there. We feasted on lovely slices of roast chicken. LeeAnn had prepared a wonderful fresh garden vegetable salad. We also had dishes of refreshing yogurt, cheese, olives and iced lemon water.

Dessert was a delight! Turkish Delight! Made for us by Ali's grandmother, "Who," Ali said, "sends her respect and greetings." Ali looked knowingly at me. I nodded.

"And now for the dessert treat made especially to help celebrate this day," and LeeAnn brought two large platters, one with a crème caramel torte and the other with a seven-layered chocolate torte.

"Iszmae heard of your predilection for chocolate and so made this confection for you, Lanny," explained Majed. "I think she likes you!"

Lanny's face turned a lovely shade of pink. Majed further explained, "It's alright, Iszmae likes everyone!" We all laughed.

"Not everyone," Iszmae declared. "I can't imagine how anyone could like that miserable rat, el-Hamin."

"He did seem to be able to attract some followers, through," commented Ed. "I don't understand it but they seem to be loyal to this guy."

"Well now," added Majed, in a conspiratorial voice, "even 'loyal' followers come to the end of their loyalty. It seems that they are quite willing to share information if the conditions are just right."

"And would the conditions have anything to do with that dark, scary room you were telling me about?" I asked.

"What room? Where? How scary?" asked Sarah, looking at Majed.

"Just an interrogation room, not to worry," reassured Majed.

"I want to know about the three figures of Jesus, Abraham and Mohammed," I asked. "Did anyone actually see them? And how did I mange to disappear?"

"I think I can help you with that," said Iszmae. "You see, the Sophia is a very old building with many additions, remodeling, passages and exits. In the dark and smoke and panic, it was not difficult for you to be carried to safety."

"By whom? Who carried me to safety?"

"I think you know the answer to that, Mom," said Sarah. I knew the subject was closed.

"And the three figures?" I asked.

"Smoke, panic, the power of suggestion, imagination and superstition. All could play a part in it," suggested Ed.

"Then again, why not Jesus, Mohammed and Abraham? Who's to say?" speculated Sarah.

"I'm still not satisfied." I said. "Something has to be behind all this."

"Mom, where's your faith?" cajoled Sarah.

"And you, baby girl," I directed at Sarah. "You've been a part of this all along, haven't you?"

Sarah came across to me and laid her hand on my arm. "Yes, Mom. We'll talk. Trust me."

I not only trusted her, I was very proud of her.

"Right, we'll talk."

"You always told me to spread my wings a bit. Well, I found out I could fly. Right now, I'm taking a bit of a hiatus from the Sisters while I get my feet wet with my new appointment to the Lester and Waterton churches. The Sisters of Sarah will keep me in touch and I'll stay in-active but connected.

So much to digest and understand.

We stayed in Istanbul for another two weeks as guests of the Ministry of Finance. We went sight seeing and visited old friends. We even had the opportunity to tour some of the many early Christian sights throughout Turkey. And we spent a good amount of time meeting with and learning about the Sisters of Sarah. What wonderful work they do!

Five days before our flight home, Sarah flew back to Minnesota, her husband, Robert, and her two churches. Robert and Sarah met while they served in the Peace Corps. Robert is a computer expert and works for a large international organization that establishes and runs homeless shelters and safe-houses.

Coincidence? I doubt it.

The day before Lanny and I flew home, with a much anticipated stop-over in London to visit our daughter, Kiri, we visited the Aya Sophia as tourists.

"You're right, Pip," said Lanny. "It does have the feel of all those souls from ages past, present still. I feel surrounded by their prayers, even today."

I looked up and thought I saw Mother Sarah and Esther walking toward us. They nodded, smiled and were gone.

"They came to say goodbye," I whispered.

"Who came? What are you whispering for?" asked Lanny.

"Never mind if you don't see them, Lan. I know they're here . . ."

Dedicated to our daughter,

Kirsten Marie

You are beautiful, brilliant,
and so talented!

Ashes, Ashes, We All Fall Down

PROLOGUE

My dad and I drove onto the campus at Wesley Seminary in Washington, D.C. I was here at last!

We got me settled in my room in Straughn Hall. I was busy unpacking and making my bed when a head popped in the doorway and said, "Hi! I'm Lemuel Sanderson. I'm on the faculty here and I hope you'll take one of my classes. Anyway, welcome." He shook my hand, introduced himself to my dad and said, "Don't worry about her, Mr. Franzen. We'll take good care of her." And with that he left.

A faculty member had actually taken the time to meet and greet me.

"It looks like this is a good place for you, Pip," said my dad.

Yes, I thought so, too. I could hardly wait to get down to the business of actually being a student. I had so much to learn!

❋ Chapter One ❋

"Ashes to ashes, dust to dust . . ." I was to have reason to remember those words two weeks after I spoke them.

My very good friend Lou Nell had died. She was a member of a small country church I had once supplied as pastor. I had been serving the larger Mount Salem United Methodist Church in Wilmington when I received a call from one of the members of Cross Roads United Church of Christ, seven miles in the country from Wilmington. They were asking if I would be interested and willing to preach at their little church. They had thirty-four members so couldn't afford a full-time pastor. Could I come and preach and make hospital calls? We went through the process (committees, District Superintendent, bishop, association, etc.) and low and behold I was installed as the part-time pastor of Cross Roads United Church of Christ.

Actually I think the people at Mount Salem were pleased as well. Many had family and friends at Cross Roads. Soon a close association arose between the two churches. That arrangement continued for the next ten years that I was appointed to Mount Salem. It continued for eight more years after I left. Now, due to some new parish alignments for Mount Salem, Cross Roads was without a pastor. That's how I happened to have been asked to have the funeral for Lou Nell.

Lou Nell had been the organist for Cross Roads Church for as long as anyone could remember. She claimed she came with the organ (it had been given as a gift by the Andrew Carnegie Foundation). No one remembered anyone but Lou Nell playing it. Of course, someone must have, just no one remembered. Anyway, Lou Nell and I became good friends and our friendship continued over the years of my ministry at Cross Roads and after that. And now I was officiating at her funeral.

The committal service was held in the little country cemetery, Whispering Pines. Lou Nell was buried next to her husband of thirty-five years. I'd had her husband, Roy's, funeral seventeen years ago.

"This body we commit to the ground, earth to earth, ashes to ashes, dust to dust, in sure and certain hope of resurrection to eternal life through Jesus Christ our Lord. Amen."

As I pat the casket I say my good byes to a wonderful, faithful friend.

Returning to the church building following the committal service we met with the wonderful scent of coffee, hot-dishes and warm rolls. Ahhh, the funeral lunch.

And friends. So many friends and family from years past up to the present. The women gave me the signal that they are ready to serve. I gather folks together and pronounce the blessing. And then, because I had come to the head of the line so I could say grace, I am obligated to serve myself, along with the family, first. (There are very few really skinny pastors and some rather large ones arising from the 'pray-er eats first' tradition.)

Dear reader, have you ever participated in a funeral lunch of a beloved member of the church? I'd almost say 'it's to die for' except that would be in poor taste.

Homemade rolls, still warm, sweet and dill pickles brought by the best pickle maker in the church (twelve grand champion ribbons at the state fair). Three different hot-dishes - Mary's rice and chicken, Sue's potatoes, vegetables and ground beef and Clara's secret (no one knows, don't ask!). Four different salads – the obligatory cole slaw, sweet the way I like it, Kathie's potato salad, Betty's fresh fruit and Melva's apricot and crème with pecans, and the dessert tray with four different kinds of brownies, one pan of six-layer bars (it's originally seven but Sandy doesn't care for coconut cream), one pan of rhubarb custard bars, one large pan of pumpkin bars with cream cheese frosting and a variety of cookies.

The food is wonderful and plentiful. But it is, after all, only the vehicle to the most important function of the funeral lunch – the stories.

Now, as we eat, everyone has opportunity to share with each other and the family the rich memories of their loved one. Let the healing begin!

We tell again the story of how Lou Nell slid from the organ bench the Sunday after Ruth Ann, the janitor, in her zeal, polished the organ bench to a high-gloss shine. That shine combined with the polyester of Lou Nell's robe nearly did her in! I had to cross the chancel and extricate her from between the organ and the bench, she sitting precariously on the pedals. Story after story was remembered and shared. Laughter rose and fell. Tears flowed freely with no embarrassment. Finally after several hours and many brownies and cups of coffee, the crowd disperses and we head for home. The funeral lunch has done its job – we remember Lou Nell as she was in life.

In the car on the way home Lanny says, "You did a good job today, Pip." I answer him, "Thanks, Lan. Your solo went well, too." We talked some more about old friends, good memories and hope that the Cross Roads church would soon have its own pastor.

"I think they're talking with the United Methodist church in Dairyville," he said. Dairyville is a small church about twenty miles away.

"That would be a good match," I said.

We drove for about ten miles.

"I'm glad we were able to get our plane tickets changed so you could do the funeral," Lanny said. "They don't usually let you do that. I think 'funeral' was the magic word that changed their minds."

"Well, it means that we'll have one less day in D.C. but it was important to be able to do the funeral," I said. "It makes a bit of a rush tonight, however."

"Not to worry," Lanny answered. "Our bags are all packed and ready. Webster is safely deposited at Sarah and Robert's. All we have to do is get in Dave and Amy's car. Pick up and delivery with a smile!"

"That's true. It was good of them to offer when they heard of our change of plans," Lanny said. We turned into the driveway at 123 Red Pine Drive. The yard light switched on as we drove up to the garage. We pulled in, parked the car and went into the house.

"It seems so quiet with no cat to greet us," he said. "I just hope he's getting along at Sarah and Robert's. Those two dogs of theirs can be pretty rough."

I snorted with laughter. 'Those two dogs' were little fluffy balls of puppy. More than likely Webster would eat them alive if they weren't careful.

"I'm going to lie down for awhile. Maybe I can get an hour or so of sleep. Then I'll get up, shower, change my clothes, and be ready to go. Before I do, do you need anything to eat?" I asked.

"No, good grief, no, I'm still full of funeral lunch," he responded.

We both lay down to snooze.

Chapter Two

We arrived in Washington on time. Our daughter, Kiri, met us at the gate and we were soon on our way to her apartment.

Kiri is our oldest daughter. After graduating with a Master's Degree from Wesley Seminary, here in D.C., she spent a year and a half in London on a work-study program. Following that she was hired by a large consortium of seminaries, graduate schools and churches to work with and teach fine arts, most particularly dance as a means of theological expression. I don't have all the specifics as to how and where this is done but I'm sure I'll pick up that information as I get acquainted with her schedule, etc. I hope I can sit in some of her classes. I'd love to watch and learn. In the meantime, I'm anxious to see her apartment and settle in for a nice vacation.

Kiri has a two bedroom apartment in the home of a widowed employee of the State Department, rather high up in the State Department I gather. The home is just off Massachusetts Avenue, just a few blocks from Wesley Seminary. It's very convenient as she has an office and most of her classes at the seminary. She does have one class at the National Cathedral on Wisconsin Avenue. Her students there are enrolled at the Cathedral School for Girls.

"I love my work. It's a dream come true. I have four classes and, of course, I need quite a bit of prep time. The class at the Cathedral is fun. The other three are fun, too. I have them in the chapel here at Wesley. There are students enrolled from five different schools. At first we thought that maybe there wouldn't be any students signed up for the course. You know, it's not a very traditional or typical seminary class. It seems to have caught on, though. I have ten students in each of the classes here and about twenty-five at the Cathedral. You should come to a class, Mom. You can come, too, Dad, but I don't think you'd be all that interested. Oh, guess what, one of my students has tickets to the Red Skins game this Sunday. Do you want to go? I said yes! They're playing the Giants," all the while maneuvering through traffic on Massachusetts Avenue. And with no warning, she turned off onto Albemarle and turned into the driveway of a lovely Georgian two-and-a-half storied home. The three-car garage door opened and in we drove. A slight, white-haired woman was waiting at the door into the house.

She greeted us warmly, introduced herself as Charlotte Belleforte, and welcomed us to Washington and to her home. Then she said, "I'm sure you'll want to unpack and rest. We'll talk later. I'm looking forward to getting to know you. It's a joy to have Kiri here with me. I feel so much safer. You must be very proud of her."

Kiri led the way up the stairs to her apartment over the garage and rear entryway. It was lovely. I could see all the personal and very individual touches that were hers.

"Here's your room," showing us a smaller bedroom off the living room. "I'm sorry, we have to share a bathroom. I've put your towels over here," pointing to bright red and gold towels. "Why don't you unpack. You can use this bureau. When you're done, I'll show you the rest of the place."

We took our time settling in our room. Afterward we met Kiri in the living room. It was small but 'cozy.' There was an eating area off the kitchen, more than ample for one person. Her bedroom was large with a nice-sized study alcove. She had a large storage area off the kitchen and a back stairway leading to the kitchen below. "Washer and dryer in the basement," Kiri said. "She doesn't charge me to use them. Actually, she says she's so glad to have someone else in the house with her that I should charge her!"

"You don't, do you?" questioned Lanny in horror.

"Of course not," replied Kiri. "But I have to admit I've got a really good deal."

Good deal, indeed! Apartment, heat, electricity, washer-dryer, garage, all for a ridiculously low price.

Mrs. Belleforte was a widow of a member of the State Department. She was a world traveler and a connoisseur of the arts.

After we talked for awhile, Kiri's phone rang.

"It's Mrs. Belleforte. She's inviting us for a light supper. She thought that we'd like an early night. This will facilitate that."

Our 'light supper' was delightful, if not terribly 'light.'

Charlotte, ("call me Charlotte, dear") had a nice meat and cheese platter, crackers, sliced fruit with dip, pickles, olives, breads and a chocolate cream pie. ("Kiri told me that Lanny loves chocolate.")

We talked of family. Kiri told more of her job. And Lanny and I spoke of our plans to be tourists at all the typical and non-typical places.

We retired to Kiri's apartment and got ready for bed.

"Thanks, Kiri, for having us. I like your apartment. Charlotte is a gem. I'm so glad you've found your way here."

"Thanks, Mom. Go ahead and use the bathroom first. Good night," and we hugged.

By the time I was ready for bed, Lanny was tucked in and sound asleep. I crawled in next to him. The bed was comfortable, warm and welcoming. Sleep was good.

❋ Chapter Three ❋

Washington, D.C. is a beautiful and interesting city. Lanny and I awoke refreshed and ready to go. Kiri had left early to get to her office and classes. We were going to 'practice' riding the Metro as arranged last evening. Charlotte was ready to drive us to the Tenly Metro station.

"Now dears, I can just as easily take you wherever you want to go," she volunteered.

"Thank you so much, Charlotte. We just might take you up on that later. But for today, we're going to experiment – no schedule, no real destination, no appointments. It's going to be a fun day of serendipity!" I answered. And off we went!

After two days of exploring and 'riding the rails' we decided we were pretty acclimated. Our travels got further afield and even more sophisticated. Instead of simply riding to the end of the line, we began getting on and off and transferring. We were quite proud of ourselves.

Friday morning came. As we sat around the table eating breakfast – I actually got up and fixed eggs, bacon, caramel rolls and juice - Kiri said, "You know, I don't have any classes today. I do have a meeting at 1:00 p.m. but that won't take too long. Why don't you come with me to the campus. You can wander around and see some of your old haunts. Afterwards we can go down to the mall or wherever you want."

"Sounds good," responded Lanny. "When do you want us to be ready?"

"Let's say about 11:00 a.m. That will give me plenty of time to answer mail and stuff before the meeting," said Kiri. "Why, did you have something you need to do before we go?"

"He has to read the newspaper from front to back," I laughed. "And there is the crossword puzzle, too. All required reading."

Lanny grinned sheepishly, "Well, someone has to do it!"

❋ Chapter Four ❋

Wesley Seminary was much the same as when I attended. The changes were subtle. Mostly new faces. Different professors. A change here. A change there.

It was, however, like coming home. I'd had such a wonderful experience as a student at Wesley.

"Where to first, Mom?" asked Kiri.

"The chapel, of course," I answered. For me, the chapel had been the center, the core of my time and my experience at Wesley. I had so many memories of high points, spiritual and emotional, in that chapel.

Named after one of the Washington-area bishops, John Trumbull Oxnard, it was a place of meeting, celebration and learning. It was also the actual final resting place of Bishop Oxnard. His ashes lay reposed in a small cask/urn placed in the floor under the center of the chancel area. Indeed, they were placed exactly under the communion table. Apparently Bishop Oxnard loved communion!

Lanny and I toured the campus, returning to the chapel at fifteen minutes to one. Kiri had time to get what she needed for her meeting. Lanny and I said we'd wait in or around the chapel. We'd meet there after her meeting and then head out to the mall and the Smithsonian.

"Pip, look at this," said Lanny. He was standing in front of the sanctuary getting a closer look at the stained glass window.

"What is it?" I asked.

"It may be my ignorance, but isn't it a bit strange to have a hack-saw and a chisel under the communion table?"

"What? Let me see," as I hurriedly made my way down the center aisle to the front. Sure enough, under the table was a pile of tools including a wrench, hammer, small hack-saw and a chisel. I also noticed that under the table, on the plaque to Bishop Oxnard's memory, there were what looked like chisel marks and scrapes.

"It looks like someone is trying to get into this," indicating the plaque/urn, said Lanny.

"Pretty sloppy workmanship," I said, thinking this might be a repair in progress. "And it looks like they left in a hurry."

"Coffee break, maybe," ventured Lanny.

"Hey, Mom, Dad. I'm ready, we can go now," said Kiri, from the back of the sanctuary.

We went to the car and were on our way to the Museum of Natural History at the Smithsonian.

Chapter Five

We had a wonderful time! I've always loved the Smithsonian. I used to go by myself and spend hours wandering from display to display. We spent time over dinner after the museum. It was late as we drove home.

"I left my notes in my office," said Kiri. "I know it's late, but do you mind if I stop at school and pick them up?"

"What's to mind?" we both agreed. "We'll wait in the car."

It was oddly dark along the side of the building. We waited for what seemed a very long time.

"What's that noise?" I asked.

"You're hearing things, Pip."

"No, I head a cry or a shout. And it's coming from inside the chapel."

"Let someone else find out. There must be someone else who can do that."

"Do you see anyone?" I asked.

"You know, now that you mention it, doesn't it seem strangely void of anyone?"

"You're right, Lan. Grab something to carry and let's go."

"Something to carry? Oh, I get it. Something to clobber someone with, you mean." Lanny fumbled around in the glove compartment until he found a flashlight. "OK, let's go."

We slowly crept into the building, following the path that Kiri had taken.

"Doesn't it seem strange that the door is unlocked?" I asked.

"Kiri had a key. She would have opened it."

"Yes, but it would have locked behind her. Unless you have that thingie that keeps it open. Someone must have left this door unlocked,"

I reasoned.

The hallway was dark, lighted only by exit lights. We headed down the hall toward the chapel, where we heard noises.

"Mom, psst, over here." We heard Kiri before we saw her.

"Thank goodness you're OK," whispered Lanny. "You are OK, aren't you?"

"Yes. Ssssh. Don't let them hear you."

"Them? Them, who?" I asked.

"Quick, get back here with me, out of the light," as she pulled us into the coat closet just off the hall.

"So here's what happened. I came in to go to my office. I heard pounding and rattling, or something, I couldn't quite tell, coming from the chapel. . ."

". . . the hack saw and chisel," mused Lanny.

"Anyway, I went to investigate. I saw two dark figures behind the communion table. It looked like they were digging or something. Then, a third figure, shorter, smaller, came out of the sacristy. It looked like he was telling the other two what to do. I was about to shout to them when Arlen Davies came into the chapel. He didn't see me. He ran down the aisle to try to get them to stop, I guess. The smaller man grabbed Arlen and clubbed him with something. I think it was a wrench. I thought he shouted something like "no, it's mine!" Then I let out a shriek or a shout. They heard me, but I don't think they saw me. I ran and hid. I stayed hidden until I heard you come in the door. I was terrified. So, what do we do now? I think they're still in there."

I thought for a moment. "Hmmm, what would a great detective do, I wonder?" I said out loud.

"Oh, do we have one here?" asked Lanny.

"We'll create a diversion, scare them. Hopefully they'll leave. We need to get to Dr. Davies as quickly as we can. First, let's call 911 and ask for help.

"Right," answered Kiri. She took out her cell and rang the number.

"Lanny, we need something that makes a loud noise."

"How about this," pointing to a fire alarm over my left shoulder.

"All right, let's go," responded Kiri.

We flipped the alarm and ran toward the chapel yelling at the top of our voices. Lanny flicked the flash light on and off and I pounded the walls as we went. Actually, we must have made a pretty silly sight. However we looked, it seemed to work. It was only a matter of a few seconds when two figures dressed in black ran out past us into the night. We quickly found the lights and hurried to where we saw Dr. Davies on the floor. His head was bloodied and his hair matted in blood and what looked like bone and brain matter. I bent over him and checked his pulse. It was very faint – I could hardly feel it. Kiri leaned over and spoke, "Arlen, Arlen, can you hear me?"

He moaned and for a moment blinked his eyes. Then he whispered, "John's ashes, all gone, all gone, lies, more lies . . ." and he stopped speaking. I could feel the breath go out from him. I heard the ambulance. Lanny had gone to show the way.

"Here, up here," I cried. They made their way toward the front of the chapel about the same time I heard the police officers come in. I leaned over Dr. Davies one last time and traced the sign of the cross on his bloody forehead.

"Rest in peace, Arlen. Rest in peace."

It was very late when the police finally released us, apparently satisfied with our explanation of what happened. "It didn't hurt that we were clean of blood spatter, as well," I muttered to myself.

Kiri actually called the president of the seminary and set in motion notification and planning of services for Arlen.

Dr. Arlen Davies, professor of Biblical Languages, had been at Wesley Seminary for twelve years. I didn't know him. Kiri said he was quiet and not too well known among the student body. So what was he doing on campus and in the chapel at this time of night? Perhaps we would never know.

We arrived at home and went to bed as fast as we could. Tomorrow would be a busy day. Today had been long and eventful.

As I drifted off to sleep a question floated past my brain. What about the third dark figure? The one who bludgeoned Davies?

❋ Chapter Six ❋

We spent the day in West Virginia. When I was in seminary, I'd served four country churches in rural Morgan County, West Virginia, as pastor. The parsonage at that time was in Berkeley Springs, West Virginia. We drove out into the countryside visiting churches and cemeteries and as many former parishioners as were home.

Two of the four churches that I had served are now closed, Oakwood Grove and Bethany. Both had been very small congregations and, although I was sad for sentimental reasons, for their closings, I could well understand the decision to close.

The two remaining churches, Green Glenn and Mount of Olives, were doing well. As a matter of fact, one of the folks we'd visited told us they were having a joint 'yard party' today at the Mount of Olives Church. We didn't want to miss it!

Mount of Olives Church sits on a ridge halfway between the Cacapon and Catoctin Mountains. It is a red brick building and shares its land with a cemetery. To the side is a wooden shed-like building that is called a 'huckster.' It has a kitchen, of sorts, and benches and tables for people to eat, sell crafts, baked goods and meals. It is the gathering place for folks to get together and celebrate a 'yard party.'

It was fun to be able to share some of my memories with Lanny and Kiri, neither of whom had been in my life when I served these churches.

We parked the car and got out. I was recognized and all heaven broke loose! Hugs, handshakes, clasps on the back, and, of course, remembrances.

We had a West Virginia, Morgan County down-home country dinner.

We had green beans with ham hocks, country ham, fried chicken, sauerkraut with pork, homemade macaroni and cheese, deviled eggs, potato salad, fried green tomatoes, sliced roast beef, scalloped corn, baked beans, tossed salad, glorified rice, sun-tea, lemonade and coffee. And we had homemade ice cream in three flavors; vanilla, fresh strawberry and chocolate. And we had homemade pie. We had coconut cream, sweet potato, apple, sour cream raisin, cherry, strawberry, chess and chocolate cream. And peaches, fresh peaches from Dale Youst's orchard.

"Now I know why you have such good memories of West Virginia, Pip," said Lanny, in between bites.

Before we left I took a walk through the cemetery.

"Saying your greetings to old friends, Pip?" asked Emma Younger.

"Yeah, kind of like that. I buried quite a few out here, you know," I answered.

"You buried my Joe," Emma said. "One of the nicest services there ever was. I'm still grateful to you."

"Thank you, Emma. It was my privilege."

"I want you to stop at the house before you go. I have a little something for you."

By the time we left, what with all the 'little somethings' folks had for me, we had a car load of goodies; a half bushel of golden delicious apples, two bags full of home-grown tomatoes, two dozen eggs, five jars of assorted homemade jams ("The berries were good this year"), four jars of homemade apple butter, two jars of honey, one jug of apple cider, two apple pies, one head of cabbage, four cucumbers and, of course, some country ham. "I remember how much you enjoyed it," said Emma. "I just happen to have some on hand. Oh yes, you'll need bread with it," handing me a loaf of homemade bread, still warm from the oven. "And you'll need mustard..."

Kiri said not to worry, she had plenty of mustard.

We hugged as we left, both Emma and I had tears in our eyes.

"Thank you so much, Emma. It was wonderful to see you again," I said.

"Thank you, Rev. Pip. I still remember you in my prayers for all you did for my Joe and me."

Later in the car Kiri said, "Wow, Mom. They really like you."

"They're wonderful, warm, caring people who took a very 'green' student pastor under their wings and taught me what it means to be in ministry. I loved them then. I still do."

We arrived at Kiri's apartment in time to share produce with Charlotte.

Mmm, fresh tomatoes for a late night snack. We all had a sandwich of country ham, homemade bread, and mustard, supplemented by apple pie, fresh cucumbers, washed down with homemade apple cider.

I almost forgot Arlen Davies.

❋ Chapter Seven ❋

The next morning we got up and went to worship at Metropolitan United Methodist Church. The service was interesting to me, especially since Wesley Seminary held its graduation ceremony there the year I was graduated. Kiri met several faculty members from Wesley. Mostly the talk was about the incident in the chapel and the death of Arlen Davies.

"You were there?" asked Dr. Louise Baxter. Dr. Baxter is professor of Old Testament Studies. "It must have been horrible. And so strange. What in the world is it all about?"

We didn't have an answer. Apparently, no one did. There were only questions.

One comment was made about the return of Bishop Oxnard's ghost. There was conversation, speculation and a good bit of skeptical laughter.

"Kiri, I hear you have tickets to the 'Skins game today," said Dr. Edward Bower, professor of Pastoral Ministries. "I don't suppose you'd rather do something else and would be able to share the tickets with poor but worthy colleagues?" he asked hopefully.

"No such luck for you, Ed. We're all going (indicating Lanny and me). Karl is picking us up in time for the kick-ff."

"Karl, Karl Who?" I asked.

"Never mind now, Mom. We have to get going if we're not going to be late." Kiri hurried us out the door and back to her apartment. We had a light lunch and changed into our 'football game' outfits (warm pants, sweaters and "please don't wear your Packers shirt, Dad"). We were waiting for Karl in plenty of time.

"So Kiri, who is Karl?" asked Lanny.

"Everyone at church seemed to know who he is. No one seemed

surprised that we were going to the game with him. Hmmm. Again I say, who is Karl?"

"He's just a friend," she responded. Lanny and I looked knowingly at each other.

"No really, we're just friends," she insisted.

"Yes, of course. We understand," I assured her.

"Mom!"

"How did you happen to meet him?" asked Lanny.

"He's a student at Wesley – part time. I don't have him in my class but we met in the library. Actually, he's a grad student at American University. He's working on a Ph.D. in Political Science with an emphasis on the economy of developing countries. Oh look, here he is. Let's go." A dark green Mercedes Benz pulled into the driveway.

Kiri made the introductions. We got in and off we went to the game. We sat in one of the VIP boxes – a first for both Lanny and me. We had a great time. The Giants won 21-13. Karl and Lanny actually watched the game. Kiri and I were busy people watching. We also pondered weighty problems. We talked about her job, her landlady and planned more sight-seeing adventures. And we wondered about Arlen Davies' murder.

"You could find out things, Mom. No one would be suspicious of a little old lady asking questions."

"Gee, thanks," I said.

"You know what I mean. You love that sort of thing. You're kind of a Jessica Fletcher type character. You look harmless enough, you innocently go in, ask questions, put two and two together, and come up with answers before the police can do a thing. It's you, Mom!"

And so it goes. I'm a harmless, innocent-looking little old lady. How do these things happen?

After the game we went out to eat and had a nice time getting to know Karl. I won't say that we 'grilled' him, but he might.

He works for the State Department. His family is well-to-do (he didn't say it that way but it wasn't hard to figure out), he's taking a class at Wesley in Contemporary Theology because it's interesting to him, he likes Kiri, and thinks the Packers are a good team. He also knows how to smooze a bit. However, Lanny was happy so that's all that really matters.

We got home about 8:45 p.m. Lanny and I went in. Kiri and Karl stayed in the car. I don't suppose they talked about the game.

"He seems nice," thought Lanny.

"His comments about the Packers didn't hurt," I mused.

"That shows he's an intelligent man. Knows how to flatter the ol' man. Not a bad idea. I'm going to take a shower and get ready for bed," he said, as he strolled toward the bedroom.

"You go ahead," I answered. "I want to watch the news."

"That's different. Usually I'm the one who watches the news. Oh, I get it. You want to see if there are anymore stories about that Davies guy."

"Good night, dear," I said and settled down in front of the TV. There wasn't much of interest on the news. There was a brief mention of the murder of Dr. Arlen Davies and that the investigation was on-going. No suspects or 'persons of interest' at this time, although there had apparently been witnesses.

Kiri came in and we went to bed.

❋ Chapter Eight ❋

Lanny and I toured Mount Vernon on Monday. Kiri let us use her car after we dropped her off at the seminary.

It's been quite a while since I've driven in D.C. so it took us a little longer to arrive back at the seminary. ("Does take your life in your own hands mean anything to you?" asked Lanny.) We parked the car. As we went into the Trott Administration Building, we noticed that the front of the sanctuary was blocked off with crime scene tape.

"I wonder if they've gotten any further toward solving Dr. Davies' death?" I asked Lanny.

"Hi," said Kiri. She came toward us from the staircase that led to her office.

"There's been a lot of hubbub around here about the murder. Everyone wants to know what happened. Actually, it's made me quite a celebrity."

"Not a good way to have your fifteen minutes of fame," responded Lanny.

"I know. I wish I could be more helpful but I really don't know anymore than what I've told them. They think Arlen just accidentally stumbled across a botched-up robbery attempt."

"I wonder," I thought out loud. I kept remembering the last words that Davies had spoken, "John's ashes, all gone . . . more lies..."

What was all gone? John's ashes? No, they were still there; I had seen them with my own eyes. And more lies? Who lied? Could someone have lied about the ashes? Something else in the cask? Some other ashes? No wait, that doesn't make sense. Did anything make sense? It all rolled around in my head until I was dizzy. Best to leave it alone and let the police solve this mystery.

I did wonder, however.

❋ Chapter Nine ❋

"Mom," in between mouthfuls of waffles and bacon, "when you were at Wesley do you ever remember stories or rumors about Bishop Oxnard's ghost? You know, was the chapel supposed to be haunted? Strange noises and all that stuff?"

We were sitting around the kitchen table having breakfast. We didn't have anything planned for the day and Kiri didn't have any classes.

"Tuesday's are good days to relax," she had said. So that's exactly what we were doing!

"Good breakfast, Kiri, Pip," said Lanny, finishing his eggs over easy and toast. "The waffles were good, too," he added. "Only problem – they make me want to go back to bed. I'm sleepy." And with that he wandered off back to bed. "I can use a little extra sleep, we've kept pretty busy," were the last things we heard him say as he disappeared into the bedroom.

"Now Mom, about this ghost story rumor," Kiri raised the question again.

"Come to think of it, I do remember that some kind of weird stories would circulate around campus every once in a while. Once it was the library stacks, occasionally it involved the refectory. Once I believe someone saw a ghostly apparition on the John Wesley and horse statue on the front lawn. Someone even thought they saw Oxnard in the laundry room. We all thought they were imagination – mostly the imagination of Bill Jeffers, the night watchman and custodian. He claimed he saw lights go on and off in the chapel, along with some other strange noises and visions. Why do you ask?"

"It seems that people have heard strange noises and seen lights go on and off in the chapel," replied Kiri. "I was just wondering if it had ever happened before. Strange, isn't it?"

"Imagination can do funny things," I said. "What triggered these 'sightings'?"

"Oh, you know, those old stories about Bishop Oxnard. All those things he was supposed to have said about never leaving Wesley and always being present, stuff like that."

"No one can actually take the ghost stories seriously," I said.

"I don't know if anyone is taking them seriously but they sure are talking about them," answered Kiri. "The library is a-buzz with stories. My guess is that some are being added to or completely fabricated on the spot!"

The phone rang. It was Charlotte asking if we needed anything from the grocery store.

"Yes, as a matter of fact, I do," responded Kiri. "How about I drive and we go together." Evidently that was fine with Charlotte. I looked in on Lanny and saw that he was fast asleep, so I left a note telling him where we were going. We met Charlotte in the garage.

"I thought we'd be better off in my car, there's more room," she said. "You drive, dear," referring to Kiri. "You know the way."

The three of us piled into Charlotte's Sedan de Ville (Cadillac, for those of you who only know Chevies and Fords), although I'm not sure it's really very appropriate to 'pile' into a de Ville. (We seated ourselves?) As we drove down Massachusetts Avenue, Charlotte suggested we stop first at a certain curio shop, "did we mind," as she was looking for just the right what-ever-it-was ("I'll know it when I see it.") for her mantel. We emerged forty-five minutes later with two bags, one large box and two trinket boxes, all bought with friends and family in mind in the wild frenzy of "tourist" shopping. Now all I have to do is remember for whom I bought.

"I'm sorry we didn't find what you were looking for, Mrs. 'B'," said Kiri.

"Never mind, dear. The fun is in the shopping, don't you think," she answered, as we pulled into the parking lot of the supermarket.

"Do you have a list?" I asked Kiri.

"Right here," she showed me the list.

"OK, let's start," as we grabbed carts and off we went.

For some reason, supermarkets in D.C. seem to have narrower aisles than what we have in Minnesota. And I missed cheese curds and a greater variety of ice cream flavors.

Charlotte was off and running with her list. You could tell that she was an expert and knew exactly what she wanted and where it was. I favor a more leisurely plan as I dart from temptation to temptation. We finally all met at the check-out counter with our full carts.

"Let's go home and have lunch," I said. "Charlotte, you'll eat with us, won't you?" We still had fresh tomatoes, cucumbers, apple pie and ham.

Sitting around the table the four of us talked about tourist sights yet to be seen.

"I definitely want to visit Arlington Cemetery. I like Arlington House and I'll want to see the changing of the guard at the tombs of the unknown soldiers. What about you, Lan?"

"Maybe we could go there tomorrow. What do you have on your schedule, Kiri?"

"I've got classes and office hours tomorrow, but I can take you to the Metro. It's pretty easy to get to Arlington from there," she answered.

"Would you like to go with us, Charlotte?" I asked.

"I'm afraid it's too much walking for me. I also have my women's book club meeting tomorrow. We've been reading Harry Potter. Can you imagine ten little old ladies sitting around discussing Harry Potter? Actually, it's quite interesting!"

After we finished our lunch and did the dishes, Lanny and I decided to take a nice walk through the neighborhood. Kiri said she had class notes to work on for tomorrow's classes. "Don't get lost, you two," she advised as we left for our walk.

D.C. is a lovely city and the neighborhood just off Massachusetts Avenue is beautiful. The homes are established and the lawns, small as they are, are manicured and colorful with flowers and landscaping. We walked for about forty-five minutes, talking, relaxing and stretching our legs.

When we arrived back at Kiri's apartment we noticed a familiar Mercedes in the driveway.

"Karl's here," observed Lanny.

"Hmmm. I don't remember visiting any of my professors at their homes while I was in seminary," I mused.

"Now Pip, be nice," answered Lanny.

"Nice? I am nice," I said. It just came to me – I used to spend time at Professor Sanderson's house. He, his wife, Martha, and I would have 'tea' together. They drank tea, I drank Dr. Pepper. It's the funny things we remember with a little reminder. We walked up the stairs to Kiri's apartment.

"Hey, you guys. Come on in. How was your walk?" asked Kiri.

"Hello, Dr. Franzen, Mr. Franzen," echoed Karl.

"Actually it is Dr. Franzen-Fielding," said Lanny, referring to me. "And I'm Mr. Fielding. But never mind. Lots of people get it wrong. We're used to it."

"Anyway, it's Pip and Lanny," I asserted. "We're pretty informal people."

"Karl has asked us to dinner and the opera at Kennedy Center," enthused Kiri. "The opera is The Marriage of Figaro. I know you like Mozart, Mom. And Karl made reservations for dinner at the Kennedy Center restaurant just in case you would like to come."

I looked at Lanny. He seemed to be in favor of the evening. We both answered together, "We'd love to. Sounds like a great evening."

"That's wonderful," said Karl. "I'm sorry this is such short notice. I was lucky enough to get tickets this morning. I've got some work to do at the office and then I'll pick you up at seven o'clock," and with that he went to the door.

"I'll see you to your car," said Kiri.

Ten minutes later Kiri still hadn't returned. Lanny speculated, "He must be having trouble getting that Mercedes started, it's taking so long."

"Now, Lan, you be good, too."

"Yes, dear. Of course, dear," he answered humbly. Too humbly, now that I think of it.

When Kiri came in she was slightly flushed and smiling.

"Have you guys got clothes you can wear tonight? We've got really good seats so we'll want to look decent. You'll need to be decent for the restaurant as well."

"I'm decent," responded Lanny.

"How about the clothes we wore to church on Sunday?" I asked. I could immediately tell her response by the frown on her face.

"Karl said you could wear one of his ties if you need to. And Mrs. 'B' has some of her husband's suits. And Mom, I've got some stuff that will look really neat on you. Come on, let's get busy!"

Lanny groaned. Kiri's eyes lit up and you could tell how we would spend our afternoon. Clearly she was on a mission.

"One question," I asked. "If we're going to dinner why is Karl picking us up at 7:00 p.m.? Doesn't the curtain go up at 8:00 p.m.? That's cutting it pretty close."

"Oh, Mom. We eat afterward." Silly me, how could I not know that. I felt the height of hick-dom.

Lanny groaned again.

"Just be sure to have a little something to eat before we go," she added.

It required quite a production just to get us ready for the production! After several false starts ("I thought the first suit I tried on was OK," and "Mom, that's not a good color for you, let's try this," and "let's have a sandwich, I'm hungry") we finally were ready and waiting at the door for our chauffer.

Lanny said, "I didn't realize looking decent involved so much work." I said, "Shhh, dear."

Mrs. 'B' (by now we were calling her that) met us with her camera.

"Smile nicely; you'll want to remember this lovely evening." We smiled. She clicked, wound and clicked again.

She whispered to Lanny, "I always did like that suit. It's so dignified. . ."

...to which Lanny murmured, "oh this old thing? Well, it's decent enough."

"... and it makes you look quite handsome, Lanny," patting him on the arm and fluffing his pocket handkerchief.

"Here's Karl now," I said. Lanny and I sat in the backseat. The soft, plush leather swallowed us up. Off we went to Foggy Bottom and the Kennedy Center.

We had a wonderful time! First of all, I love the Kennedy Center.

The three theater venues all in one, the halls of nations and states and the huge head of John Kennedy all sparked memories of the years I had attended events here. The opera house is my favorite. We were seated in the dress circle – no wonder Kiri wanted us to look decent!

The Waterford crystal lights gleamed and then dimmed. The huge seamless curtain opened and we were gifted with a wonderful performance of Figaro! I love Mozart and 'Voi, Che Sapita' is one of my favorite Mozart areas.

Our meal after the opera was all we had anticipated. Lanny and I had fresh salmon with lemon and tossed green salad. For dessert we all had baked Alaska. It was wonderful!

It was a mild fall evening. As we drove home, Karl opened the sun roof; at this time of night it became the moon roof, and we all enjoyed the night air. We were all still enjoying the combination of Mozart, a lovely meal and pleasant conversation as we drove past Wesley Seminary on our way home.

"Stop, Karl!" exclaimed Kiri.

"What? What's the matter?" he answered.

"Pull over, turn in, I saw something in the chapel," insisted Kiri.

"I did too, but I just thought it was my overly-active imagination," I added.

Karl drove around Wesley Circle and turned back toward American University. He turned right into the seminary driveway and came to a stop alongside of the administration building that houses the chapel. We waited.

"Well, do you see anything?" asked Karl.

"Not now, but I was sure I saw something," she repeated.

"I'm up for it. Have you got your keys?" This I directed at Kiri.

"Yup, let's go!" as she got out of the car and headed toward the side entrance. I followed as quickly as I could, disengaging myself from the back-seat plushness. As I got out I saw Karl and Lanny looking at each other with the same kind of 'here we go again. What we don't have to put up with' look.

Car doors slammed as Lanny and Karl followed Kiri and me.

"How do you live with this?" asked Karl.

"Balance," answered Lanny. "I've learned to balance some of

the impetuous craziness against the meals, family and fun we have together."

"I'll have to try that," murmured Karl.

"Also," paused Lanny. . .

"Yes?" waited Karl. . .

"Love helps. It makes it all come together," philosophized Lanny.

"Got it," replied Karl, nodding his head.

By this time, Kiri had opened the door and she and I were stealthfully creeping down the hallway toward the chapel. Behind us I could hear Lanny and Karl following us, loudly 'shushing' each other the whole way.

"You two sound like The Three Stooges," I complained.

"But there's only two of us," remarked Lanny. "Say, we must be pretty good!"

"Great, by now you two. . ."

". . .stooges. . ."added Karl, with a snicker.

"Have made enough noise to scare the dead. You've warned them that we're here and frightened them off!" She sounded disappointed.

"Exactly our point," concluded Karl.

"A man after my own heart," responded Lanny, clapping Karl on the shoulder.

During all this conversation we'd turned on the lights and walked down the aisle of the chapel. We ended up standing next to the pulpit and in front of the communion table.

"No one here," I said.

"No, but look, someone was here." There were dusty footprints beneath the table. It looked as if someone had been drilling in the marble slabs that made up the flooring.

"And look here," Karl said. He leaned over and picked up a large flashlight.

"Someone was here, working in the dark," speculated Lanny.

"Hmmm, ghosts don't need flashlights," I whispered to no one in particular. "And they don't leave footprints."

❀ Chapter Ten ❀

When we got home, Kiri called the seminary president and told him what we had found.

"We didn't disturb anything so there might be fingerprints or whatever. I don't know if you want to call the police. You know there's probably some kind of connection. . . Yes, alright. . . good night," and left it at that.

"Good night, Karl. Thank you for a really lovely evening," I said. Lanny seconded that with, "Good night, Moe."

We both went to bed.

❋ Chapter Eleven ❋

We slept later than we had planned, but were moving about and taking nourishment by 8:00 a.m. Lanny and I prepared for a day at Arlington National Cemetery.

"Fanny pack."

"Check."

"Disposable camera."

"Check."

"Kleenex."

"Check."

"Oh, for goodness sake. You act like you're going to the North Pole!" exclaimed Kiri.

"We have to plan carefully. Us old geezers need to take nothing for granted," chuckled Lanny.

"Oh you guys," she said, laughingly. "Be sure you have enough cash. No one takes checks anymore."

"Yes, we know. We're all ready whenever you are," I responded, finishing packing our lunch.

It was a beautiful fall day with temperatures in the mid-60's. There was a lovely blue sky and a mild, warm breeze. Perfect! Kiri dropped us off at the Tenley Metro Station where we would board the subway and head for Arlington.

"I'll meet you here at 4:30 p.m. OK?" she asked. We synchronized our watches. I usually don't wear one, but had made an exception for today and was wearing the Cinderella watch I'd gotten at Disneyworld several years ago. We said our good-byes and started down the huge, cavernous hole that would take us to the Red Line and eventually to Arlington.

Arlington National Cemetery is a very popular tourist sight anytime, but today it seemed especially busy. I'm sure the beautiful weather attracted them as it had us. Lanny and I took in all the places we wanted to see, spending our time first at the Custis-Lee (or Arlington House) Mansion. I love to stroll among the lovely old trees and, concurrently, the Civil War tombstones that surround the mansion. The view from the front porch overlooking Washington is spectacular.

We took our time, sitting and enjoying the weather and the ambiance of this very special place, filled with history.

We caught the tram and rode it to the 'Unknowns.' There is always a crowd there, at least during the daylight hours. We arrived with about ten minutes to spare for the changing of the guard. Looking at the faces of those around me, I can see I'm not the only one who is moved by the ceremony. We stand and watch.

A crowd of schoolchildren had gathered to my right. Several of them are loudly talking, snickering, laughing and chewing and blowing bubblegum. Where are their teachers, I wonder. No matter, the sergeant at arms walks over to them, gives them a steelie look and says, "This is the Tomb of the Unknown Soldiers. We honor them and show respect. You will not dishonor them or yourselves with disrespectful behavior. You will be quiet. You will swallow your gum. You will stand at attention. You will give your full honor to those who have given their full measure for our country. Is that understood?"

I heard gulps and one or two whispered, "Yes sirs."

For some reason, I felt vindicated.

The students lowered their heads and were silent for the rest of their time there. Perhaps we'd all learned a lesson. I presume several students had.

We spent time wandering along the rows and rows of white markers. We visited the Kennedy graves. We "remembered the Maine." We found a lovely, quiet grove with a bench and ate our lunch of country ham sandwiches, cheese, and an apple for me and a chocolate bar for Lanny. We sat and thought. And we just sat. I looked at my watch. It was almost 2:45 p.m.

"Oops, better start heading back," I said.

"I guess so, but it's so nice and peaceful here," answered Lanny. We sat for a minute or two more then headed toward the Visitor's Center and restrooms. Then the walk to the Metro tracks and home.

It had been a lovely day.

❋ Chapter Twelve ❋

We rode the escalator up from the subway level to street level. I tried to look back but it only made me dizzy and I lost by balance. Lanny caught me. "Easy does it, Pip."

"Wow, that's about fifty gazillion feet down there," I said.

"Oh, Pip, you always exaggerate. I think it's only ten gazillion," he laughed. Whatever it is, it's very deep and high.

Kiri was waiting for us at the top.

"I'm glad you're right on time," she said. "The memorial service for Arlen is tonight at 7:00 p.m. in the chapel. I thought you'd like to go."

We went to the car and drove home. Both Lanny and I were glad for the opportunity to sit and rest our feet for a moment. Following a quick shower, a change of clothes and a light supper, we were ready to go in plenty of time to get a good parking space at the seminary.

The service was in the chapel. As we entered, I saw there were many seminary community members gathering as well. Apparently, these folks had been Arlen Davies only 'family.' The front of the sanctuary had two floral arrangements placed side by side of the cremains urn.

We found a place to sit toward the back of the sanctuary. The service itself was simple, dignified and short. There were two congregational hymns sung. They are two of my favorites, "For All the Saints," and the communion hymn, "Here, O My Lord I See Thee."

Singing those hymns in that very special place brought memories flooding over me. I remembered worship services I had been part of years ago as a student. I recalled several plays I had directed for the community. I remembered the time we stayed up most of the night waiting for the 'ghost of Oxnard' to show up. We'd hidden in various places in the chapel so we could observe and surprise the 'ghost.' Now where did that memory come from, I wondered. I drifted back to reality and the conclusion of the memorial service as I heard the familiar words, "ashes to ashes, dust to dust. . ." and remembered Lou Nell. I remembered Emma's Joe and all the other friends and strangers I had buried. And now, Arlen, "ashes to ashes . . ."

The benediction was pronounced, the postlude was played (Widor's Toccata! My favorite!), and we all began to leave, most of us walking toward the refectory for a reception and 'funeral lunch,' and a time of fellowship.

While folks were busily talking and sharing conversation, I took the opportunity to slip out and return to the empty chapel. I walked down the aisle and stood at the communion table. I knelt over the plaque in the floor. Although it had obviously been cleaned and polished, you could still see the marks and scrapes that had been made by the murderers.

Arlen's last words, "John's ashes," and "lies, all lies," came to mind. Were the ashes gone? What if he didn't mean the ashes? What else might be missing from the cremains urn? Another word flashed across my mind. Not urn or cask but 'safe-deposit' box. Could it be possible that something else had been placed there for 'safe-keeping'? But what? And why?

"Excuse me, can I help you?" came from the back of the sanctuary. I looked up and saw Dr. Lance Shockley, my 'old' worship professor.

"Pip, Pip Franzen, is that you?" he asked.

"Hello, Dr. Shockley. It's good to see you," I answered. We met midway down the aisle and shook hands.

"Are you here for the memorial service? I remember now, you were the one who discovered him, didn't you? That must have been terrible."

We talked for a few moments and then I said, "I'd better get back to the reception. I left my family there."

"That's right. Your daughter, Kiri, is on our faculty. She's making a real creative impact on our ideas of worship and communicating theology. And she's also put Wesley on the map for cutting edge worship curriculum. You must be very proud, Pip."

"Yes, I'm proud of both my girls," and I told him a bit about Sarah, as well.

We shook hands again, made a few comments about the memorial service which he had led, and parted.

I walked along the tunnel between the two buildings on my way to the refectory and the reception. I saw him walking toward me before he saw me. Actually I was really surprised to see him because I thought he'd died about five years ago!

"Dr. Acheson, how nice to see you!" I exclaimed.

Dr. Richard Acheson was on the faculty when I was a student at Wesley. He seemed ancient then. As a matter of fact, he had retired while I was here. He taught Historical Techniques of Interpreting Scripture and was a bit of a curmudgeon even then. I don't believe he was very well liked, except by Arlen Davies, who was sort of his 'pet.' Davies death must have been hard on him.

Dr. Acheson seemed not to see my extended hand. For that matter, he seemed not to see me. He tottered past me. I didn't give up. "Wasn't Dr. Davies your student?" I asked.

"My student. Yes. A damn good one, too" he answered. "He was more than that. He was a partner. A business partner," he said wryly and wandered away toward Trott Administration Building.

"Goodness. A business partner. How odd. I wonder what he meant by that?" I thought. I walked to the refectory and met with Kiri and Lanny. Karl had joined us, as well.

"We're ready to go, Mom. How about you?"

It had been a long, busy day. And the bed felt wonderful.

❀ Chapter Thirteen ❀

One of my favorite places in D.C. is the National Cathedral and grounds. I love to wander through the gardens, find a nook and watch the squirrels run from tree to tree. Lanny and I were sitting and relaxing when we saw a little black squirrel come scampering toward us. He (gender being pretty indeterminate in a rapidly moving squirrel) stopped about ten feet from us.

"Look, he's trying to decide if we're friendly or not," said Lanny.

"We'd better smile so he'll know," I said. "Isn't he cute?"

The squirrel, henceforth known as Blackie, timidly hopped toward us. Slowly I reached in my pocket and drew out a piece of bread crust. And no, I don't usually carry bread crust in my pocket. This one was leftover from an earlier breakfast on the run and no waste receptacles.

I held the crust out toward Blackie. He waited. I waited. We eyed each other. And then he sauntered up to me, rose on his hind legs and took the bread. Then instead of running off to hide the bread, he jumped onto the bench beside me, hunched down, and proceeded to eat his meal, chattering the whole time.

Lanny and I sat very still watching with amazement at this, one of God's smaller creatures, eating his lunch and, in general, just enjoying life.

After Blackie finished his meal, he lifted his front paw, gently touched me on my arm and was off to whatever new adventure was his.

I love the cathedral – its beautiful, vaulted ceilings, the great organ, the many nooks and crannies, the gift shop in the lower level, the Bishop's chair, the choir, the crossing and all the many memorial plaques and various chapels. My favorite chapel is The Children's Chapel, made in miniature to fit the sizes of younger worshippers.

And yet I must confess my very favorite memory when I think of that huge and impressive Cathedral is Blackie, the friendly squirrel.

❋ Chapter Fourteen ❋

That same night we were again back at the chapel on Wesley's campus. I was hidden in the balcony overlooking the chapel. Lanny was in the hallway coat alcove on the first floor and Kiri had secreted herself somewhere in the sanctuary among the pews.

Why, one might ask, are we in such a ridiculous position? Because Kiri heard voices. More particularly, she heard voices saying that they would "try again tomorrow, midnight should be late enough . . ."

And where did those voices come from?

"I heard them in the basement hallway right after the funeral, Mom. I'm pretty sure they weren't talking about meeting for pizza."

So here we are, hidden, wearing dark clothes, armed with flashlights and waiting. And, Lanny would add, "feeling pretty silly."

It was 12:23 a.m. according to my trusty Cinderella watch. Perhaps the 'suspects' were only going for pizza after all. Everything was dark with only the illumination of the occasional 'EXIT' light. It was quiet, too. I was sure I would give away my presence by my loud breathing! Then I heard it. I could hear the recognizable clicking of the side door being opened. Then footsteps, strangely echoing on the tile floor leading to the chapel. I saw lights shining – like beams of flashlights and then heard voices.

"So where is the old geezer? He was supposed to meet us here," said one.

"He's so old he probably forgot or fell asleep, whatever. . ."

"I believe you gentlemen mean me," came a third voice from the sacristy, to the right of the communion table. A dark figure followed the voice as Dr. Richard Acheson emerged from the doorway. In one hand he held a flashlight. In the other hand he held what looked to me from across the distance to be a gun. Hmmm, apparently not all seminary professors are pacifists!

"You killed Arlen but you won't get me," he insisted loudly.

"The key, old man. Give me the key," said one of the two.

"No, lift out the box, hand it to me. If you do what I ask, I'll see to it that you get your pay-off. Otherwise, I shall have to shoot both of you," demanded Acheson.

"You and what army, old man? You don't have the guts to shoot us," snarled one of the men.

While this battle of wits was playing out before us, I was struggling with one of my own. Do we make ourselves known? Yell? Scream? Sit quietly? What is the best course of action in an impossible situation such as this?

Just as I was about to decide, I heard an enormous groan, or moan, sailing out over the entire chapel. Lights blinked on, then off and a huge glowing white figure appeared on the wall immediately behind the communion table. I knew it wasn't Halloween yet so what could this be? Some sort of prank gone insidiously wrong? As I was pondering the question, I heard an eerie voice emanating from – where?

"You betrayed me, Richard. You kept the money for your own selfish use. I will have my sweet revenge. You may think you buried me in that box, but I am able to get to you at anytime," and then silence and darkness.

"Bishop Oxnard?" I whispered.

I could hear the two men with Acheson drop what they had and run down the aisle and out the door.

Lanny and I ran toward Acheson at the same time he crumbled to the floor moaning and clutching his chest.

"Kiri, call 911," I called as we reached him.

As she came toward us, she switched on the lights. Then we saw Acheson withering on the floor. I leaned over him, taking the flashlight and revolver from his hands.

"Richard, can you hear me?" I asked.

His eyes fluttered open and he gazed at the space over my left ear.

I reached for the pulse at his throat and could barely feel it.

"Richard," I urged again. "Can you tell me who those two men are?"

"I've called 911. They're on their way."

"None too soon," I thought out loud. "It's getting to be a habit.

Acheson groaned. Lanny knelt down and supported his head.

"My heart . . . pills in my pocket . . help me," he muttered.

Quickly I reached into his vest pocket. There was a small bottle labeled 'Nitroglycerin'. I opened the bottle and emptied two of the small pills onto the palm of my hand and helped him put them under this tongue. Acheson seemed to relax a bit. He beckoned me to lean close to him.

"Don't know who you are. . .Oxnard left papers. . .money. . .couldn't cash them in – hid them. . .thought they'd be safe. . .someone else knew. . .all gone. . .poor John. . .all gone. . ." he coughed and dropped his head back, closing his eyes.

The paramedics arrived and worked on him, eventually placing him on a gurney and loading him into the ambulance.

As the ambulance left, the police officers arrived. We told them the story.

"And why were you here at midnight?" asked the officer.

We carefully went over the events of the night again and again.

"You mean to tell me you came here, hid in the dark waiting for you don't know what, on the strength of over-hearing voices saying they would try again at midnight?" asked Detective O'Neal, the lead officer on this case.

"That's about it, officer." responded Kiri.

"But why? That's next to nothing to go on. Or at least, why didn't you call the police?" he asked.

"Would you have believed her?" I responded. "I mean, after all, here we are in the midst of evidence and us as eye witnesses and you still don't believe us," I asserted.

"Mom," cautioned Kiri.

"Easy does it, Pip," added Lanny.

"Well it does seem strange that Dr. Acheson has to be carted off in an ambulance, scared into what is probably a heart attack and we three all attest to the fact that there were two other people here, apparently involved in an earlier crime; murder, in fact, and in spite of all this, we're the ones being questioned," I argued.

Both Kiri and Lanny were hiding their faces. I think they were waiting for the other shoe to drop and me to loose it completely.

"I think you're probably right, ma'am," answered Detective O'Neal. "And you've got spunk, as well."

We slithered out the door, our legs too weak and shaky to properly carry us, and drove back to Kiri's apartment.

"I don't know how you do it, Pip," said Lanny.

"Me either, Mom. I would have been terrified to say those things."

"Not me," I twinkled. "I've got spunk!"

I will admit that it took about an hour for my legs to stop shaking after I got into bed.

❋ Chapter Fifteen ❋

The fact of the matter is the police, on the strength of our testimony or not, did follow through, finding finger prints of two unidentified persons. They also found a projection device that would explain the ghostly apparition and electrical equipment for voice magnification. In other words, Oxnard's ghost.

Detective O'Neal called the next morning to let us know what they found. He also called, he said, to pass along greetings from his brother-in-law, Ed Arnold. Ed is one of the members of law enforcement who worked with me on the WE Experience in Istanbul. (See Sisters of Sarah.)

"It's a small world, isn't it, Detective," I laughed.

"Call me Allen," he responded. "I have a request to make of you. Can you nose around on campus, kind of see who Acheson knew when he was on the faculty. What was his relationship with Oxnard and Davies, that sort of thing?"

I said I would see what I could find. "How is Dr. Acheson, anyway?"

"He died about an hour ago," he replied.

"I'm so sorry. Was it a heart attack as I suspected?" I asked.

"That isn't very clear. The pills that were labeled "Nitroglycerin" were actually something quite different. Someone tampered with his medication. Actually, it looks like someone committed murder."

We talked for a few more minutes and then, "Greet Ed for me, Allen," and we hung up. I told Lanny of my conversation with Allen.

"He's really related to Ed Arnold? No wonder he listened to you last night. So, what are your next steps?"

"I think I'll be doing some homework at the library. Allen said he would clear the way for me to work in the 'stacks' and some of the older records that are usually not open to the general student body."

I knew exactly where I would look. I remembered when I was a student I'd read a booklet about the sale of some prime property with the proceeds directed to the building and re-location of the then Westminster Seminary from its first site in rural Maryland to its new identification and location as Wesley Seminary in Washington, D.C. I think I'll look there.

❋ *Chapter Sixteen* ❋

I found it! Or at least I found evidence of what I was looking for. Way back in the stacks I found the pamphlet that I had read so many years ago. It described an island in the St. Lawrence River. On the island was a 'large summer home' and varied out buildings. The property had been deeded to Westminster Seminary. The seminary had consequently sold the property and used the money from the sale to support the new campus in Washington, D.C. I remember that at the time I read the description, I thought the island and buildings would have been a great retreat center for the school. However, the money from the sale facilitated the sale and move to D.C.

As I was looking over the pamphlet with its description and dimensions of the island I noticed something else for the first time. On the corner of the last page there was a mark. No, not so much a mark as a puncture, the kind that would be made by a staple. Apparently there had been at least one other page in this file. I wonder. . .

I went back to the file cabinet where I found this file. I noticed that the manila folder it had been in was titled, "Former Gifts, Properties." I opened the folder. There on the bottom, torn and crumpled, was a small piece of paper with a staple in it. I took it out and read it.

"The Skyler Properties
Fifty acres of vacant lot,
to be sold..."

Could this be connected in some way to Acheson, the killing of Arlen Davies, and Bishop Oxnard's ashes?

I carefully put the file folder and paper in my notebook and quietly left the library.

I knew exactly where to go to get the information I needed. Dr. Lemuel Sanderson knew everyone and everything that had anything to do with Westminster/Wesley Seminary. He had been on the faculty for more than fifty years and was still active at age ninety-seven. He and his wife, Martha, had a small home a block or two from the seminary. I phoned and yes, he'd be delighted to talk with me. Why didn't I come over and we could have tea with our conversation.

It was a pleasant walk to the Sanderson home. The trees had begun to turn to their fall colors. There was a crispness in the air that hadn't been there earlier.

Martha Sanderson answered my knock with, "Pip, it's so nice to see you after all these years." I was amazed she remembered me! "Lem is in the study. Come on through. I'll bring refreshments in just a moment. Now let me see. Lem will have tea, I'll have lemonade. And, if I remember correctly, you like Dr. Pepper." Amazing! How in the world did she know that?

I went into the study and shook hands with Dr. Sanderson. We sat down and made small talk. Martha brought a tray with tea, lemonade and a cold glass of Dr. Pepper. The tray also had a plate of my favorite frosted sugar cookies.

"Pip, have a cookie with your drink," offered Dr. Sanderson. I took a cookie and ate it with relish.

"Now," continued Dr. Sanderson, "let's get down to business. You're here about the very sad deaths of our colleagues, Arlen and Richard. And you're trying to find connections between the two and all the mischief surrounding John Oxnard's little crypt."

I brought him up-to-date regarding all I knew about the deaths of Davies and Acheson.

As I finished he said, "Let me see the scrap of paper you found in the file."

I showed him the 'Skyler' paper.

"I remember Jonas Skyler. He was a wealthy businessman in Westminster. He was a little odd. He had some strange ideas about seminary education and put some rather restrictive mandates on his gifts to the seminary. We had to sort of 'dance around' some of them. What happened was that he wanted all seminarians to be over thirty, male and white. We talked him out of the age and gender requirements but he was firm about the race issue. He often made monetary gifts to the seminary. There was a rumor that he had a plot of land he wanted to dump for a tax shelter. It was about fifty acres on the northwest corner of D.C. It wasn't worth much."

"So the seminary turned him down?" I asked.

"Officially, the seminary refused further donations from Skyler."

"You say 'officially.' Is there another side to this issue?" I questioned him.

"You understand, of course, that you didn't hear this from me and what I'm about to tell you never really happened."

I nodded my understanding. Now we were getting to the nitty-gritty.

Sanderson took a sip of tea. He began.

"Officially we never received anymore gifts from Skyler. In actuality, we were given several gifts of cash that simply disappeared into the general budget listed under various departments. We were also offered property. Which we, of course, according to our policy, refused.

However, the deed to the property was received by various members of the faculty. Supposedly they were holding it in trust, whatever they meant by that. Bishop Oxnard discovered the discrepancy in policy and in fact. I've always personally wondered at his sudden heart attack and death. He was cremated and his ashes placed in the chapel named for him. Buried, I suspect, with the sales receipt from the property. Incidentally, that property was sold to the federal government as the site for the new CIA building. I would suppose the sale would have been close to two million dollars. The situation now is probably a struggle between those who are left or those who somehow found out about all these illegal and unethical transactions. A struggle that must be quite confrontational."

My brain was whirling with all these new speculations.

"But if both Davies and Acheson are gone, who's left?" I puzzled out loud.

"The one who planned and controlled the whole thing," he responded. "Or else someone found out about it and is now the one left who knows."

"Well, do you know who that is?" I asked.

"One can only speculate," he answered. He folded his arms on his desk and would say no more.

We chatted a bit more about the world, the seminary and about our families. Then I said, "I've taken enough of your time. Thank you for your help and your opinions," and proceeded to make my way to the front door. Martha was at the door to say good-bye.

"It has been so nice to see you again, Pip. I do so remember with pleasure all the times we spent in the library together." (We had both worked in the library for a time. (She as a research/resource librarian and me as the general flunkie.) As I was going out the door, she handed me a little box.

"I've put some of those cookies you like so much in here. They're for you and your family to enjoy. It was a pleasure to see you again." And with that, the door was closed. Amazing, so hospitable and so curt all at once. Oh well, she was ninety-four, after all and allowed some mood swings.

I had a lot to think about as I walked back to the campus. Who stood to gain? Who had access to Acheson and his pills? Why open the cremains vault now? And, incidentally, how did Martha know about my liking her cookies? And why, now, would she pack a little box of them? I'd not said anything. I opened the box. There was about two dozen frosted sugar cookies neatly wrapped in a large paper napkin. And underneath the napkin there was a note in precise Spencerian hand.

"Pip, Lem is not always what he seems. His facts are accurate. But he's left important information out of his story. Please be very careful.

In memory of happier days, I remain, affectionately yours,
Martha Agnes Hensile Sanderson"

She signed her full legal name to a little note like this? Then I remembered. When we worked together at the library she would occasionally sign her name thusly. I'd asked her, "Why do you sign your name Martha Sanderson one time and Martha Agnes Hensile Sanderson another?"

"Well dear, that's to remind me of the importance of the material. It's my own little code for serious, pay attention to and so on. Whenever I sign my full name then you know I mean business. Now hush, this can be our own little secret."

Martha was indeed sharing her concern regarding the seriousness of my visit and conversation with Sanderson.

❋ *Chapter Seventeen* ❋

Allen O'Neal phoned later that evening. He said they'd been able to pull finger prints from the equipment that projected the 'ghost.'

"It's two students from American University. They got a call from someone who told them what to do and when. Arranged for them to get inside the building. Told them it was a 'theological job,' you know, a play on the 'Holy Spirit.' Anyway, they were each paid five hundred dollars in cash. No money trail there. We've interrogated them pretty carefully and their story holds up. At least we know how and why of the 'ghost' presence and the voice."

"Are these two the same ones responsible for Arlen Davies' death?"

"It seems as if we have two different sets of two, if you know what I mean. Luckily for us we were able to get some skin cells off of the wrench that hit Davies. As I speak, a team of officers is on their way to make an arrest of two brothers-for-hire. They've been involved in lots of suspicious activities. Both have rap sheets as long as your arm. I think the DNA on this one will be enough to catch them. In each case, however, you realize that we only have the hired help."

I told him about the 'Skyler property' but didn't reveal my source.

"I can do some digging in Deeds and Records. I'll get back to you on this. Thanks, Pip, err, Dr. Franzen-Fielding, err, Dr. Pip. Say, what do people call you, anyway," he stuttered.

"Mostly just Pip. Some call me Dr. Pip. Whatever you're comfortable with," I suggested.

"What does Ed call you?" he asked.

"Dr. Pip or just Pip," I answered.

"Pip it is," and then, "I'll check on a few things and get back to you. Good night."

Chapter Eighteen

I didn't sleep well that night. Could Dr. Sanderson know more than he told me about this case? For that matter, what, if anything, is his involvement? Dr. Sanderson involved in something underhanded and unethical? Nonsense, not the Dr. Sanderson I knew and revered.

I tossed and turned until I finally got up and went to the living room so I wouldn't wake Lanny. Two thoughts cross-crossed my mind. The first was that Dr. Sanderson couldn't possibly have anything to do with the deaths of Davies and Acheson. And also, didn't he hint at an unnatural and premature death of Bishop Oxnard? No, of course not. This was my over-active imagination at work again.

The other thought was opposite. Who else was around all those many years ago. And who is still around. Only one man, Sanderson. And what about Martha's note? Much as I hate to admit it, I think I'm stuck with the latter and not the former scenario. After I made the decision to suspect Lemuel Sanderson the pieces began to fall into place. He shared an office with Acheson until just recently. They both taught one class on campus until last semester. He knew Bishop Oxnard well. He was on the faculty both at Westminster and Wesley. He had free access to various files relating to the Skyler properties. Indeed he seemed very familiar with them. Davies was a protégé of Acheson who was a protégé of Sanderson? And he was the last one left.

So the question was what happened to the money? And how much money?

After an hour or so of ruminating these theories I was able to go back to bed and to sleep.

Lanny, however, it seems, was wide awake.

Chapter Nineteen

I met Allen for breakfast at the refectory on campus. He had a good bit more information.

"Actually, it was easy, Pip," he explained. "Once we had a clue as to where to look, the puzzle pieces fell into place. A deed for fifty acres of land was registered in Jonas Skyler's name. It was then signed over to Lemuel Sanderson for Westminster Seminary. The papers then say that a Westminster Seminary doesn't exist..."

"Wow. By now it had ceased to exist and had become Wesley. But shouldn't that have been duly noted?"

"Apparently someone 'forgot' to follow up on some paper work."

"Ah, yes. OK. Right. A case of very carefully planned timing. And also a pretty big risk that no one would investigate the last paper trail of Westminster into Wesley," I concluded.

"Anyway," said Allen, "the property was placed in trust to said Dr. Lemuel Sanderson until such time as a decision could be reached as to what should happen."

"Let me guess," I speculated. "After a few years it was decided to deed the property over to Sanderson."

"Absolutely correct," asserted Allen.

"And no one objected or questioned it? Nothing was done to look into this? It was that easy?"

"A paper was signed and attested to by two witnesses..."

"Dr. Richard Acheson and Dr. Arlen Davies, by any chance?" I asked.

"Right, only Davies wasn't a 'Dr.' yet. He was a student at Wesley Seminary."

"How exemplary," I added.

"One day after the deed was transferred to Sanderson's name, the property was sold to the United States government as a site for the CIA building and properties. Sale price was two million five hundred thousand dollars. The money trail seems to lead us to several bank accounts in Switzerland."

"Goodness, now I remember several continuing education seminars both Sanderson and Acheson would attend with regularity. They were in Geneva."

"To be close to the money, no doubt," suggested Allen.

"Is there anyway Bishop Oxnard's death could be investigated?" I asked.

"Pretty doubtful," he answered. "You can't exhume ashes."

"What about hospital records? Could there be hints in them?"

"Pip, he died at home and was pronounced dead by a next-door neighbor who happened to be an M.D. Lemuel Sanderson called him. He was cremated the next day."

"What does the death certificate say was the cause of death?" I asked.

"Simple. He died of heart failure."

"Doesn't everyone?" I asked.

"That's pretty hard to disagree with. And very hard to prove otherwise, especially when the body is cremated almost immediately."

"I guess the most we can say is that this death was certainly convenient. If he had questions about what was going on, he never had a chance to ask them. When did he die?"

"Two days after the deed was transferred. And yes, his death would have been very convenient. It created a diversion on campus. Not much of anything was done or discussed for several weeks after his death and memorial service," explained Allen.

"I have to hand it to you Allen. You certainly came up with some interesting information. It pretty much points to Sanderson for fraud and murder. What about the two brothers you said were going to be picked up? Did anything come of that?"

"As a matter of fact it did. They pointed to Sanderson. Said he wanted to 'clear the boards,' apparently his exact words. They were to get rid of Davies. They were willing to talk if they could cut a deal. They'll go to jail for a long time, but at least they won't be charged with murder one. Once we started probing, everything pretty much led back to Sanderson."

"How did Dr. Sanderson leave all this evidence behind? I mean the set-up seems so clever."

"He didn't realize that he had," said Allen. "He thought all the evidence was safely locked in the box that held Oxnard's ashes. And that, he figured, was carefully and safely buried in the chapel. Who would think of digging that up, he must have reasoned."

"So why did it get opened? And who opened it first? Acheson and Davies? What happened? Maybe someone got greedy. Maybe a little bit of blackmail?"

"Probably right, Pip. We won't know for sure unless we can get Sanderson to talk."

As it happened, the opportunity to talk with Dr. Sanderson came shortly after that.

I received a call from him.

"Pip, I realize that I left our conversation hanging in the air. I'd like to rectify that. Won't you stop over this afternoon about 1:30 and we'll have tea, some of Martha's crumpets (he chuckled) and conversation."

"That sounds good to me. I'll look forward to seeing you," and I hung up the phone. I immediately called Allen and told him of this new development.

"I'm not sure how I feel about your going there by yourself. There's too much at stake for him."

We ended up outfitting me with a tiny microphone-recorder hidden in my bra and connected to Allen, who would be waiting outside Sanderson's home. The microphone was small but itchy. I tried not to scratch, especially not where the microphone was placed.

One thirty came and I knocked on the front door of Lemuel and Martha's home. Martha answered my knock.

"Oh, hello dear. And did you enjoy the cookies?" she asked meaningfully.

"Yes, they were wonderful," I said, seeing Lemuel around the corner. "My husband, Lanny, has a sweet tooth. He certainly was glad for them. Thank you, again."

"Come in, Pip," inserted Dr. Sanderson. He ushered me into his office. I sat down across from his large mahogany desk. Whereas his desk had been cluttered with piles and stacks of papers and file folders when I'd been here before, today his desk was almost clear with the exception of one of two folders. He watched me eyeing them.

"Yes, my dear. I've cleared my desk of all the inconsequential things. I've invited you here to finish up some business from a very long time ago. You see, I do remember you as a student. While you weren't the most brilliant scholar (he grinned) you were tenacious. You didn't give up on things. Remembering that, I knew I couldn't just leave things hand in the air. It's probably just as well. This has gone on long enough."

As he finished his sentence, Martha knocked, then came in carrying a tray.

"I thought you would both be ready for some refreshments," she said, as she set the tray on the end of the desk. "I know you'll have tea, Lem. I've got a new kind. I hope you'll like it. It's called 'Sunset Glory' or some such thing. I've tried it and didn't like it much. But you're so much more knowledgeable about these things, dear. I hope you'll like it. And I have iced Dr. Pepper for you, Pip, dear. And I put out some of the cookies you like. Please enjoy your tea time," and she was gone.

Sanderson sipped his tea and said, "Martha hovers over me so. She is a good wife to me, however. Quite obedient," and poured himself another cup of 'Sunset Glory.' This isn't too bad," he sipped again. "A little sharp but not too bad. Poor Martha, she never did learn to appreciate the finer things. Now, to business. Where were we?"

"You'd cleared your desk and I was not brilliant but tenacious," I answered.

"Yes, and you always were a bit sarcastic, I believe. Well, never mind now." And with that he pulled an evil looking revolver from his desk drawer and pointed it at me.

"I almost hate to do this. You have been a worthy adversary. Well, it can't be helped," he sighed.

"If you're going to do away with me anyway," I said.

"Very perceptive of you, my dear," he added.

"Won't you at least answer some questions? Just for my satisfaction, of course," I said. And for Allen O'Neal's edification, I thought. And incidentally, Allen, now might be a good time to put in an appearance.

"Yes, I suppose you deserve that much, at least," he said, somewhat wearily, I thought.

He proceeded. "Jonas Skyler had more money that was good for him. He was also very racially prejudiced. Excuse me," and he coughed. "We worked it out that he would donate to the seminary on the understanding that no Black would benefit. Easy enough in those days. We didn't have many Black students. The land deal was my idea, after all. He didn't need it or the money from it."

"How much money did you actually realize?" I asked.

"From the sale of the land? Two-and-a-half million. From the other little gifts and donations he made that supposedly went to the seminary? Oh, I'd say about seven million."

My mouth dropped.

"You didn't know about them, did you? Well you do now, much good it will do you," he laughed and then began to cough sharply. He appeared to be having difficulty catching his breath.

"To continue," he said, his voice very raspy now.

"Did Bishop Oxnard know? Was he involved?" I asked.

"Old strait-laced Oxnard? He snooped around asking questions. Then he put two and two together. . ."

"So you killed him," I speculated.

"He had to go. Don't worry, we did it humanely. He didn't suffer, much, anyway," he laughed again, this time gasping for breath.

"And the money? Where is it now?" I asked.

"Some of it's been spent, expenses, you know. But I have most of it here from the accounts that we had it in Switzerland."

And with that he retrieved a leather carrying case from behind his desk.

"There's ten million dollars here what with interest and the little bit I've spent. Arlen and Richard wanted their share of it. Their share! How dare they! This is my money. I earned every cent of it!" He became louder and louder, pounding his desk and waving the gun about. I weaved and ducked in response.

"And if you shoot me, how will you explain that or get rid of my body?" hoping to buy some time as I alert Allen.

"Arlen can dispose of you. He's quite good at that," he rambled, breathlessly.

"Oh, how many bodies have there been?" I asked curiously.

"There are no bodies, you idiot," he shouted at me. "There's only ashes. Ashes, ashes, we all fall down," he answered in a high-pitched, sing-songie voice.

"What will you do with all that money, Lemuel?" I asked quietly.

"Why, keep it, of course. We're going to build a new seminary, you know. We'll need a library. Yes, that's it. A library. Martha would like that," he broke off, coughing and gasping for air.

The door opened. Allen? I hoped.

Martha came across to Sanderson and cajoled him to be seated. She set the revolver aside, on his desk. Then she knelt beside him, soothing him with soft, endearing words.

"That's good, dear. Quiet down. Rest now. You've had a long day. A long, good life. Time for you to rest. Let the tea work its magic. Close your eyes. Breathe deeply. Sit back, all will be well." Martha was in charge now. She looked at me and nodded.

"It's time, Lemuel. It's past time. You don't really want to harm our dear Pip. She was such a good student. She used to come to tea, too, dear."

I gradually realized what was happening.

"You put poi. . ."

"Yes, dear. I had to. It's time for him to be done with all the wrong and mistakes he caused. It all began as a game, I believe. He just wanted to know if he could do it. But then it grew; one thing led to another. People got hurt, Lemuel got in deeper. You see, I know Lemuel – the real Lemuel. He was deeply affected and surprised by his greed. It's been working on him all these years. I've watched him changed over time. He has become the evil that he enacted – dark, nefarious, cunning and mad. It's been like watching Dorian Grey. I will miss him, but then, he's actually been gone to me for over twenty years."

"And now, oh dear," she continued, as she saw Sanderson slump over the desk. Clearly the poison had done its work quickly, efficiently and effectively, "and now you have another murderer on your hands."

She rubbed her hands together and leaned over the kissed Sanderson on the forehead.

"Good-bye my dear. You are in the hands of a gentler justice."

I put my arms around her, holding her close.

❀ Chapter Twenty ❀

They held a joint memorial service for both Richard Acheson and Lemuel Sanderson.

"It's appropriate, I think, don't you, Pip?" They were involved in so many of the same things," declared Martha.

"Yes, I guess they were," responded Dr. Harvey Taylor, professor of New Testament Literature. "I guess I didn't realize how close they were, that's all,' he added.

"Closer than you know," answered Martha.

Dr. Lemuel Sanderson's cause of death has been listed as heart failure. And with a prompt from me, so had Dr. Acheson's death. Dr. Arlen Davies death is 'death by misadventure by person or persons unknown' and is still an open case. I believe it will remain that way.

Much to the surprise of many of the seminary community, Martha asked that I have the service. Acheson had no family, so she said she thought it would be OK with him.

Lanny and I stayed three extra days so that I could do so. Both Richard and Lemuel were cremated.

"...Ashes, to ashes, dust to dust..."

We have come full circle.

EPILOGUE

Lanny and I returned to 123 Red Pine Drive. It was good to be home. Sarah brought Webster back. He scolded us for leaving him. I could have sworn he sucked in his cheeks to look emaciated and ill-used.

"Oh, for goodness sake, Dad. He was perfectly happy until he saw you. What a drama-cat!"

Three weeks later we received a call from Kiri.

"Mom, Martha is gone. She died early this morning. Karl and I were with her at her home. It looked like a heart attack, the doctor said. She'd been having a nice, warming cup of tea. . ."

"Sunset Glory," I asked.

"Yes, I asked her if I could have some but she said she was finishing up the last of it. I was to be sure to tell you that, whatever that means."

So we have come to the end. The rest of the millions was donated, willed by Martha, to the seminary for use as scholarships and the library and whatever else they should decide.

Oh yes, she also willed me $500,000 as a token of friendship and enduring love. "In memory of the good times," she said in her letter, and signed it "Martha Agnes Hensil Sanderson."

And Kiri and Karl? Well, that's up to them, isn't it?